Does man's future have a stop?

a wandering dead star from outside
the galaxy—
the insects take over—
a new ice-age—
or just plain super-enormous
fission, fusion, fission bomb??????

"No" says Tenn. "4 times no!!!!
The future belongs to man!"

But what will man do with it?

Ah! that's Tenn's secret—and yours when
you read these 4 prophetic novelettes

Time in Advance

BANTAM BOOKS • NEW YORK

time
in
advance

WILLIAM TENN

TIME IN ADVANCE

A BANTAM BOOK
PUBLISHED JUNE 1958

Copyright Notices and Acknowledgements

FIREWATER reprinted from Astounding Science Fiction by permission of Street & Smith Publications, Inc. Copyright, 1952, by Street & Smith Publications, Inc.

THE SICKNESS reprinted from Infinity Science Fiction by permission of Royal Publications, Inc. Copyright, 1955, by Royal Publications, Inc.

TIME IN ADVANCE reprinted from Galaxy Science Fiction Magazine by permission of Galaxy Publishing Corporation. Copyright, 1956, by Galaxy Publishing Corporation.

WINTHROP WAS STUBBORN reprinted from Galaxy Science Fiction Magazine by permission of Galaxy Publishing Corporation. Copyright, 1957, by Galaxy Publishing Corporation.

Back cover photograph by Aurea Keyes

PRINTED IN THE UNITED STATES OF AMERICA

BANTAM BOOKS, 25 West 45th Street, New York 36, New York

Contents

Firewater

The hairiest, dirtiest and oldest of the three visitors from Arizona scratched his back against the plastic of the webfoam chair. "Insinuations are lavendor nearly," he remarked by way of opening the conversation.

His two companions—the thin young man with dripping eyes, and the woman whose good looks were marred chiefly by incredibly decayed teeth—giggled and relaxed. The thin young man said "Gabble, gabble, honk!" under his breath, and the other two nodded emphatically.

Greta Seidenheim looked up from the tiny stenographic machine resting on a pair of the most exciting knees her employer had been able to find in Greater New York. She swiveled her blond beauty at him. "That too, Mr. Hebster?"

The president of Hebster Securities, Inc., waited until the memory of her voice ceased to tickle his ears; he had much clear thinking to do. Then he nodded and said resonantly, "That too, Miss Seidenheim. Close phonetic approximations of the gabble-honk and remember to indicate when it sounds like a question and when like an exclamation."

He rubbed his recently manicured fingernails across the desk drawer containing his fully loaded Parabellum. Check. The communication buttons with which he could summon any quantity of Hebster Securities personnel up to the nine hundred working at present in the Hebster Building lay some eight inches from the other hand. Check. And there were the doors here, the doors there, behind which his uniformed bodyguard stood poised to burst in at a signal which would blaze

1

before them the moment his right foot came off the tiny spring set in the floor. *And* check.

Algernon Hebster could talk business—even with Primeys.

Courteously, he nodded at each one of his visitors from Arizona; he smiled ruefully at what the dirty shapeless masses they wore on their feet were doing to the calf-deep rug that had been woven specially for his private office. He had greeted them when Miss Seidenheim had escorted them in. They had laughed in his face.

"Suppose we rattle off some introductions. You know me. I'm Hebster, Algernon Hebster—you asked for me specifically at the desk in the lobby. If it's important to the conversation, my secretary's name is Greta Seidenheim. And you, sir?"

He had addressed the old fellow, but the thin young man leaned forward in his seat and held out a taut, almost transparent hand. "Names?" he inquired. "Names are round if not revealed. Consider names. How many names? Consider names, *reconsider* names!"

The woman leaned forward too, and the smell from her diseased mouth reached Hebster even across the enormous space of his office. "Rabble and reaching and all the upward clash," she intoned, spreading her hands as if in agreement with an obvious point. "Emptiness derogating itself into infinity—"

"Into duration," the older man corrected.

"Into infinity," the woman insisted.

"Gabble, gabble, honk?" the young man queried bitterly.

"Listen!" Hebster roared. "When I asked for—"

The communicator buzzed and he drew a deep breath and pressed a button. His receptionist's voice boiled out rapidly, fearfully:

"I remember your orders, Mr. Hebster, but those two men from the UM Special Investigating Commission are here again and they look as if they mean business. I mean they look as if they'll make trouble."

"Yost and Funatti?"

"Yes, sir. From what they said to each other, I think they know you have three Primeys in there. They asked me what are you trying to do—deliberately inflame the Firsters? They said they're going to invoke full supranational powers and force an entry if you don't—"

"Stall them."

"But, Mr. Hebster, the *UM Special Investigating*—"

"Stall them, I said. Are you a receptionist or a swinging door? Use your imagination, Ruth. You have a nine-hundred-

2

man organization and a ten-million-dollar corporation at your disposal. You can stage any kind of farce in that outer office you want—up to and including the deal where some actor made up to look like me walks in and drops dead at their feet. Stall them and I'll nod a bonus at you. *Stall them.*" He clicked off, looked up.

His visitors, at least, were having a fine time. They had turned to face each other in a reeking triangle of gibberish. Their voices rose and fell argumentatively, pleadingly, decisively; but all Algernon Hebster's ears could register of what they said were very many sounds similar to *gabble* and an occasional, indisputable *honk!*

His lips curled contempt inward. Humanity prime! *These* messes? Then he lit a cigarette and shrugged. Oh, well. Humanity prime. And business is business.

Just remember they're not supermen, he told himself. *They may be dangerous, but they're not supermen. Not by a long shot. Remember that epidemic of influenza that almost wiped them out, and how you diddled those two other Primeys last month. They're not supermen, but they're not humanity either. They're just different.*

He glanced at his secretary and approved. Greta Seidenheim clacked away on her machine as if she were recording the curtest, the tritest of business letters. He wondered what system she was using to catch the intonations. Trust Greta, though, she'd do it.

"Gabble, honk! Gabble, gabble, gabble, honk, honk. Gabble, honk, gabble, gabble, honk? Honk."

What had precipitated all this conversation? He'd only asked for their names. Didn't they use names in Arizona? Surely, they knew that it was customary here. They claimed to know at least as much as he about such matters.

Maybe it was something else that had brought them to New York this time—maybe something about the Aliens? He felt the short hairs rise on the back of his neck and he smoothed them down self-consciously.

Trouble was it was so *easy* to learn their language. It was such a very simple matter to be able to understand them in these talkative moments. Almost as easy as falling off a log— or jumping off a cliff.

Well, his time was limited. He didn't know how long Ruth could hold the UM investigators in his outer office. Somehow he had to get a grip on the meeting again without offending them in any of the innumerable, highly dangerous ways in which Primeys could be offended.

He rapped the desk top—gently. The gabble-honk stopped short at the hyphen. The woman rose slowly.

3

"On this question of names," Hebster began doggedly, keeping his eyes on the woman, "since you people claim——"

The woman writhed agonizingly for a moment and sat down on the floor. She smiled at Hebster. With her rotted teeth, the smile had all the brilliance of a dead star.

Hebster cleared his throat and prepared to try again.

"If you want names," the older man said suddenly, "you can call me Larry."

The president of Hebster Securities shook himself and managed to say "Thanks" in a somewhat weak but not too surprised voice. He looked at the thin young man.

"You can call me Theseus." The young man looked sad as he said it.

"Theseus? Fine!" One thing about Primeys when you started clicking with them, you really moved along. But *Theseus!* Wasn't that just like a Primey? Now the woman, and they could begin.

They were all looking at the woman, even Greta with a curiosity which had sneaked up past her beauty-parlor glaze.

"Name," the woman whispered to herself. "Name a name."

Oh, no, Hebster groaned. *Let's not stall here.*

Larry evidently had decided that enough time had been wasted. He made a suggestion to the woman. "Why not call yourself Moe?"

The young man—Theseus, it was now—also seemed to get interested in the problem. "Rover's a good name," he announced helpfully.

"How about Gloria?" Hebster asked desperately.

The woman considered. "Moe, Rover, Gloria," she mused. "Larry, Theseus, Seidenheim, Hebster, me." She seemed to be running a total.

Anything might come out, Hebster knew. But at least they were not acting snobbish any more: they were talking down on his level now. Not only no gabble-honk, but none of this sneering double-talk which was almost worse. At least they were making sense—of a sort.

"For the purposes of this discussion," the woman said at last, "my name will be . . . will be—My name *is* S.S. Lusitania."

"Fine!" Hebster roared, letting the word he'd kept bubbling on his lips burst out. "That's a *fine* name. Larry, Theseus and . . . er, S.S. Lusitania. Fine bunch of people. Sound. Let's get down to business. You came here on business, I take it?"

"Right," Larry said. "We heard about you from two others who left home a month ago to come to New York. They talked about you when they got back to Arizona."

4

"They did, eh? I hoped they would."

Theseus slid off his chair and squatted next to the woman who was making plucking motions at the air. "They talked about you," he repeated. "They said you treated them very well, that you showed them as much respect as a thing like you could generate. They also said you cheated them."

"Oh, well, Theseus," Hebster spread his manicured hands. "I'm a businessman."

"You're a businessman," S.S. Lusitania agreed, getting to her feet stealthily and taking a great swipe with both hands at something invisible in front of her face. "And here, in this spot, at this moment, so are we. You can have what we've brought, but you'll pay for it. And don't think you can cheat us."

Her hands, cupped over each other, came down to her waist. She pulled them apart suddenly and a tiny eagle fluttered out. It flapped toward the fluorescent panels glowing in the ceiling. Its flight was hampered by the heavy, striped shield upon its breast, by the bunch of arrows it held in one claw, by the olive branch it grasped with the other. It turned its miniature bald head and gasped at Algernon Hebster, then began to drift rapidly down to the rug. Just before it hit the floor, it disappeared.

Hebster shut his eyes, remembering the strip of bunting that had fallen from the eagle's beak when it had turned to gasp. There had been words printed on the bunting, words too small to see at the distance, but he was sure the words would have read *E Pluribus Unum.* He was as certain of that as he was of the necessity of acting unconcerned over the whole incident, as unconcerned as the Primeys. Professor Kleimbocher said Primeys were mental drunkards. But why did they give everyone else the D.T.'s?

He opened his eyes. "Well," he said, "what have you to sell?"

Silence for a moment. Theseus seemed to forget the point he was trying to make; S.S. Lusitania stared at Larry.

Larry scratched his right side through heavy, stinking cloth.

"Oh, an infallible method for defeating anyone who attempts to apply the *reductio ad absurdum* to a reasonable proposition you advance." He yawned smugly and began scratching his left side.

Hebster grinned because he was feeling so good. "No. Can't use it."

"Can't use it?" The old man was trying hard to look amazed. He shook his head. He stole a sideways glance at S.S. Lusitania.

She smiled again and wriggled to the floor. "Larry still isn't talking a language you can understand, Mr. Hebster," she cooed, very much like a fertilizer factory being friendly. "We came here with something we know you need badly. Very badly."

"Yes?" *They're like those two Primeys last month,* Hebster exulted: *they don't know what's good and what isn't. Wonder if their masters would know. Well, and if they did—who does business with Aliens?*

"We . . . have," she spaced the words carefully, trying pathetically for a dramatic effect, "a new shade of red, but not merely that. Oh, *no!* A new shade of red, and a full set of color values derived from it! A complete set of color values derived from this one shade of red, Mr. Hebster! Think what a non-objectivist painter can do with such a—"

"Don't sell me, lady. Theseus, do you want to have a go now?"

Theseus had been frowning at the green foundation of the desk. He leaned back, looking satisfied. Hebster realized abruptly that the tension under his right foot had disappeared. Somehow, Theseus had become cognizant of the signal-spring set in the floor; and, somehow, he had removed it.

He had disintegrated it without setting off the alarm to which it was wired.

Giggles from three Primey throats and a rapid exchange of "gabble-honk." Then they all knew what Theseus had done and how Hebster had tried to protect himself. They weren't angry, though—and they didn't sound triumphant. Try to understand Primey behavior!

No need to get unduly alarmed—the price of dealing with these characters was a nervous stomach. The rewards, on the other hand—

Abruptly, they were businesslike again.

Theseus snapped out his suggestion with all the finality of a bazaar merchant making his last, absolutely the last offer. "A set of population indices which can be correlated with—"

"No, Theseus," Hebster told him gently.

Then, while Hebster sat back and enjoyed, temporarily forgetting the missing coil under his foot, they poured out more, desperately, feverishly, weaving in and out of each other's sentences.

"A portable neutron stabilizer for high altit—"

"More than fifty ways of saying 'however' without—"

". . . So that every housewife can do an *entrechat* while cook—"

". . . Synthetic fabric with the drape of silk and manufactura—"

6

"... Decorative pattern for bald heads using the follicles as—"

"... Complete and utter refutation of all pyramidologists from—"

"All right!" Hebster roared, "*All right!* That's enough!"

Greta Seidenheim almost forgot herself and sighed with relief. Her stenographic machine had been sounding like a centrifuge.

"Now," said the executive. "What do you want in exchange?"

"One of those we said is the one you want, eh?" Larry muttered. "Which one—the pyramidology refutation? That's it, I betcha."

S.S. Lusitania waved her hands contemptuously. "Bishop's miters, you fool! The new red color values excited him. The new—"

Ruth's voice came over the communicator. "Mr. Hebster, Yost and Funatti are back. I stalled them, but I just received word from the lobby receptionist that they're back and on their way upstairs. You have two minutes, maybe three. And they're so mad they almost look like Firsters themselves!"

"Thanks. When they climb out of the elevator, do what you can without getting too illegal." He turned to his guests. "Listen—"

They had gone off again.

"Gabble, gabble, honk, honk, honk? Gabble, honk, *gabble,* gabble! Gabble, honk, gabble, honk, gabble, honk, honk."

Could they honestly make sense out of these throat-clearings and half-sneezes? Was it really a language as superior to all previous languages of man as . . . as the Aliens were supposed to be to man himself? Well, at least they could communicate with the Aliens by means of it. And the Aliens, the Aliens—

He recollected abruptly the two angry representatives of the world state who were hurtling towards his office.

"Listen, friends. You came here to sell. You've shown me your stock, and I've seen something I'd like to buy. *What* exactly is immaterial. The only question now is what you want for it. And let's make it fast. I have some other business to transact."

The woman with the dental nightmare stamped her foot. A cloud no larger than a man's hand formed near the ceiling, burst and deposited a pailful of water on Hebster's fine custom-made rug.

He ran a manicured forefinger around the inside of his collar so that his bulging neck veins would not burst. Not right now, anyway. He looked at Greta and regained confidence from the serenity with which she waited for more conversation to transcribe. There was a model of business precision for you. The Primeys might pull what one of them had in London two years ago, before they were barred from all metropolitan areas—increased a housefly's size to that of an elephant—and Greta Seidenheim would go on separating fragments of conversation into the appropriate shorthand symbols.

With all their power, why didn't they *take* what they wanted? Why trudge wearisome miles to cities and attempt to smuggle themselves into illegal audiences with operators like Hebster, when most of them were caught easily and sent back to the reservation and those that weren't were cheated unmercifully by the "straight" humans they encountered? Why didn't they just blast their way in, take their weird and pathetic prizes and toddle back to their masters? For that matter, why didn't their masters— But Primey psych was Primey psych—not for this world, nor of it.

"We'll tell you what we want in exchange," Larry began in the middle of a honk. He held up a hand on which the length of the fingernails was indicated graphically by the grime beneath them and began to tot up the items, bending a digit for each item. "First, a hundred paper-bound copies of Melville's 'Moby Dick.' Then, twenty-five crystal radio sets, with earphones; two earphones for each set. Then, two Empire State Buildings or three Radio Cities, whichever is more convenient. We want those with foundations intact. A reasonably good copy of the 'Hermes' statue by Praxiteles. And an electric toaster, *circa* 1941. That's about all, isn't it, Theseus?"

Theseus bent over until his nose rested against his knees.

Hebster groaned. The list wasn't as bad as he'd expected—remarkable the way their masters always yearned for the electric gadgets and artistic achievements of Earth—but he had so little time to bargain with them. *Two* Empire State Buildings!

"Mr. Hebster," his receptionist chattered over the communicator. "Those SIC men—I managed to get a crowd out in the corridor to push toward their elevator when it came to this floor, and I've locked the . . . I mean I'm trying to . . . but I don't think—Can you—"

"Good girl! You're doing fine!"

"Is that all we want, Theseus?" Larry asked again. "Gabble?"

Hebster heard a crash in the outer office and footsteps running across the floor.

8

"See here, Mr. Hebster," Theseus said at last, "if you don't want to buy Larry's *reductio ad absurdum* exploder, and you don't like my method of decorating bald heads for all its innate artistry, how about a system of musical notation—"

Somebody tried Hebster's door, found it locked. There was a knock on the door, repeated most immediately with more urgency.

"He's *already* found something he wants," S.S. Lusitania snapped. "Yes, Larry, that was the complete list."

Hebster plucked a handful of hair from his already receding forehead. "Good! Now, look, I can give you everything but the two Empire State Buildings and the three Radio Cities."

"*Or* the three Radio Cities," Larry corrected. "Don't try to cheat us! Two Empire State Buildings *or* three Radio Cities. Whichever is more convenient. Why . . . isn't it worth that to you?"

"Open this door!" a bull-mad voice yelled. "Open this door in the name of United Mankind!"

"Miss Seidenheim, open the door," Hebster said loudly and winked at his secretary who rose, stretched and began a thoughtful, slow-motion study in the direction of the locked panel. There was a crash as of a pair of shoulders being thrown against it. Hebster knew that his office door could withstand a medium-sized tank. But there was a limit even to delay when it came to fooling around with the UM Special Investigating Commission. Those boys knew their Primeys and their Primey-dealers; they were empowered to shoot first and ask questions afterwards—as the questions occurred to them.

"It's not a matter of whether it's worth my while," Hebster told them rapidly as he shepherded them to the exit behind his desk. "For reasons I'm sure you aren't interested in, I just can't give away two Empire State Buildings and/or three Radio Cities with foundations intact—not at the moment. I'll give you the rest of it, and—"

"Open this door or we start blasting it down!"

"Please, gentlemen, please," Greta Seidenheim told them sweetly. "You'll kill a poor working girl who's trying awfully hard to let you in. The lock's stuck." She fiddled with the door knob, watching Hebster with a trace of anxiety in her fine eyes.

"And to replace those items," Hebster was going on. "I will—"

"What I mean," Theseus broke in, "is this. You know the

9

greatest single difficulty composers face in the twelve-tone technique?"

"I can offer you," the executive continued doggedly, sweat bursting out of his skin like spring freshets, "complete architectural blueprints of the Empire State Building and Radio City, plus five . . . no, I'll make it ten . . . scale models of each. And you get the rest of the stuff you asked for. That's it. Take it or leave it. Fast!"

They glanced at each other, as Hebster threw the exit door open and gestured to the five liveried bodyguards waiting near his private eletor. *"Done,"* they said in unison.

"Good!" Hebster almost squeaked. He pushed them through the doorway and said to the tallest of the five men: "Nineteenth floor!"

He slammed the exit shut just as Miss Seidenheim opened the outer office door. Yost and Funatti, in the bottle-green uniform of the UM, charged through. Without pausing, they ran to where Hebster stood and plucked the exit open. They could all hear the elevator descending.

Funatti, a little, olive-skinned man, sniffed. "Primeys," he muttered. "He had Primeys here, all right. Smell that unwash, Yost?"

"Yeah," said the bigger man. "Come on. The emergency stairway. We can track that elevator!"

They holstered their service weapons and clattered down the metal-tipped stairs. Below, the elevator stopped.

Hebster's secretary was at the communicator. "Maintenance!" She waited. "Maintenance, automatic locks on the nineteenth floor exit until the party Mr. Hebster just sent down gets to a lab somewhere else. And keep apologizing to those cops until then. Remember, they're SIC."

"Thanks, Greta," Hebster said, switching to the personal now that they were alone. He plumped into his desk chair and blew out gustily: "There must be easier ways of making a million."

She raised two perfect blond eyebrows. "Or of being an absolute monarch right inside the parliament of man?"

"If they wait long enough," he told her lazily, "I'll *be* the UM, modern global government and all. Another year or two might do it."

"Aren't you forgetting one Vandermeer Dempsey? His huskies also want to replace the UM. Not to mention their colorful plans for you. And there are an awful, awful lot of them."

"They don't worry me, Greta. *Humanity First* will dissolve overnight once that decrepit old demagogue gives up the ghost." He stabbed at the communicator button. "Mainte-

10

nance! Maintenance, that party I sent down arrived at a safe lab yet?"

"No, Mr. Hebster. But everything's going all right. We sent them up to the twenty-fourth floor and got the SIC men re-routed downstairs to the personnel levels. Uh, Mr. Hebster—about the SIC. We take your orders and all that, but none of us wants to get in trouble with the Special Investigating Commission. According to the latest laws, it's practically a capital offense to obstruct 'em."

"Don't worry," Hebster told him. "I've never let one of my employees down yet. The boss fixes everything is the motto here. Call me when you've got those Primeys safely hidden and ready for questioning."

He turned back to Greta. "Get that stuff typed before you leave and into Professor Kleimbocher's hands. He thinks he may have a new angle on their gabble-honk."

She nodded. "I wish you could use recording apparatus instead of making me sit over an old-fashioned click-box."

"So do I. But Primeys enjoy reaching out and putting a hex on electrical apparatus—when they aren't collecting it for the Aliens. I had a raft of wire and tape recorders busted in the middle of Primey interviews before I decided that human stenos were the only answer. And a Primey may get around to bollixing them some day."

"Cheerful thought. I must remember to dream about the possibility some cold night. Well, I should complain," she muttered as she went into her own little office, "Primey hexes built this business and pay my salary as well as supply me with the sparkling little knicknacks I love so well."

That was not quiet true, Hebster remembered as he sat waiting for the communicator to buzz the news of his recent guests' arrival in a safe lab. Something like ninety-five per cent of Hebster Securities had been built out of Primey gadgetry extracted from them in various fancy deals, but the base of it all had been the small investment bank he had inherited from his father, back in the days of the Half-War—the days when the Aliens had first appeared on Earth.

The fearfully intelligent dots swirling in their variously shaped multicolored bottles were completely outside the pale of human understanding. There had been no way at all to communicate with them for a time.

A humorist had remarked back in those early days that the Aliens came not to bury man, not to conquer or enslave him. They had a truly dreadful mission—to ignore him!

No one knew, even today, what part of the galaxy the Aliens came from. Or why. No one knew what the total of

11

their small visiting population came to. Or how they operated their wide-open and completely silent spaceships. The few things that had been discovered about them on the occasions when they deigned to swoop down and examine some human enterprise, with the aloof amusement of the highly civilized tourist, had served to confirm a technological superiority over Man that strained and tore the capacity of his richest imagination. A sociological treatise Hebster had read recently suggested that they operated from concepts as far in advance of modern science as a meteorologist sowing a drought-struck area with dry ice was beyond the primitive agriculturist blowing a ram's horn at the heavens in a frantic attempt to wake the slumbering gods of rain.

Prolonged, infinitely dangerous observation had revealed, for example, that the dots-in-bottles seemed to have developed past the need for prepared tools of any sort. They worked directly on the material itself, shaping it to need, evidently creating and destroying matter at will!

Some humans had communicated with them—

They didn't stay human.

Men with superb brains had looked into the whirring, flickering settlements established by the outsiders. A few had returned with tales of wonders they had realized dimly and not quite seen. Their descriptions always sounded as if their eyes had been turned off at the most crucial moments or a mental fuse had blown just this side of understanding.

Others—such celebrities as a President of Earth, a three-time winner of the Nobel Prize, famous poets—had evidently broken through the fence somehow. These, however, were the ones who didn't return. They stayed in the Alien settlements of the Gobi, the Sahara, the American Southwest. Barely able to fend for themselves, despite newly-acquired and almost unbelievable powers, they shambled worshipfully around the outsiders speaking, with weird writhings of larynx and nasal passage, what was evidently a human approximation of their masters' language—a kind of pidgin Alien. Talking with a Primey, someone had said, was like a blind man trying to read a page of Braille originally written for an octopus.

And that these bearded, bug-ridden, stinking derelicts, these chattering wrecks drunk and sodden on the logic of an entirely different life-form, were the heavy yellow cream of the human race didn't help people's egos any.

Humans and Primeys despised each other almost from the first; humans for Primey subservience and helplessness in human terms, Primeys for human ignorance and ineptness in Alien terms. And, except when operating under Alien orders and through barely legal operators like Hebster, Primeys didn't communicate with humans any more than their masters did.

When institutionalized, they either gabble-honked themselves into an early grave or, losing patience suddenly, they might dissolve a path to freedom right through the walls of the asylum and any attendants who chanced to be in the way. Therefore the enthusiasm of sheriff and deputy, nurse and orderly, had waned considerably and the forcible incarceration of Primeys had almost ceased.

Since the two groups were so far apart psychologically as to make mating between them impossible, the ragged miracle-workers had been honored with the status of a separate classification:

Humanity Prime. Not better than humanity, not necessarily worse—but different, and dangerous.

What made them that way? Hebster rolled his chair back and examined the hole in the floor from which the alarm spring had spiraled. Theseus had disintegrated it—*how?* With a thought? Telekinesis, say, applied to all the molecules of the metal simultaneously, making them move rapidly and at random. Or possibly he had merely moved the spring somewhere else. Where? In space? In hyperspace? In time? Hebster shook his head and pulled himself back to the efficiently smooth and sanely useful desk surface.

"Mr. Hebster?" the communicator inquired abruptly, and he jumped a bit, "this is Margritt of General Lab 23B. Your Primeys just arrived. Regular check?"

Regular check meant drawing them out on every conceivable technical subject by the nine specialists in the general laboratory. This involved firing questions at them with the rapidity of a police interrogation, getting them off balance and keeping them there in the hope that a useful and unexpected bit of scientific knowledge would drop.

"Yes," Hebster told him. "Regular check. But first let a textile man have a whack at them. In fact let him take charge of the check."

A pause. "The only textile man in this section is Charlie Verus."

"Well?" Hebster asked in mild irritation. "Why put it like that? He's competent I hope. What does personnel say about him?"

"Personnel says he's competent."

"Then there you are. Look, Margritt, I have the SIC run-

13

ning around my building with blood in its enormous eye. I don't have time to muse over your departmental feuds. Put Verus on."

"Yes, Mr. Hebster. Hey Bert! Get Charlie Verus. Him."

Hebster shook his head and chuckled. These technicians! Verus was probably brilliant and nasty.

The box crackled again: "Mr. Hebster? Mr. Versus." The voice expressed boredom to the point of obvious affectation. But the man was probably good despite his neuroses. Hebster Securities, Inc., had a first-rate personnel department.

"Verus? Those Primeys, I want you to take charge of the check. One of them knows how to make a synthetic fabric with the drape of silk. Get that first and then go after anything else they have."

"Primeys, Mr. Hebster?"

"I said Primeys, Mr. Verus. You are a textile technician, please to remember, and not the straight or ping-pong half of a comedy routine. Get humping. I want a report on that synthetic fabric by tomorrow. Work all night if you have to."

"Before we do, Mr. Hebster, you might be interested in a small piece of information. There is *already* in existence a synthetic which falls better than silk—"

"I know," his employer told him shortly. "Cellulose acetate. Unfortunately, it has a few disadvantages: low melting point, tends to crack; separate and somewhat inferior dyestuffs have to be used for it; poor chemical resistance. Am I right?"

There was no immediate answer, but Hebster could feel the dazed nod. He went on. "Now, we also have protein fibers. They dye well and fall well, have the thermoconductivity contol necessary for wearing apparel, but don't have the tensile strength of synthetic fabrics. An *artificial* protein fiber might be the answer: it would drape as well as silk, might be we could use the acid dyestuffs we use on silk which result in shades that dazzle female customers and cause them to fling wide their pocketbooks. There are a lot of *ifs* in that, I know, but one of those Primeys said something about a synthetic with the drape of silk, and I don't think he'd be sane enough to be referring to cellulose acetate. Nor nylon, orlon, vinyl choloride, or anything else we already have and use."

"You've looked into textile problems, Mr. Hebster."

"I have. I've looked into everything to which there are big gobs of money attached. And now suppose you go look into those Primeys. Several million women are waiting breathlessly for the secrets concealed in their beards. Do you think, Verus, that with the personal and scientific background I've

14

just given you it's possible you might now get around to doing the job you are paid to do?"

"Um-m-m. Yes."

Hebster walked to the office closet and got his hat and coat. He liked working under pressure; he liked to see people jump up straight whenever he barked. And now, he liked the prospect of relaxing.

He grimaced at the webfoam chair that Larry had used. No point in having it resquirted. Have a new one made.

"I'll be at the University," he told Ruth on his way out. "You can reach me through Professor Kleimbocher. But don't, unless it's very important. He gets unpleasantly annoyed when he's interrupted."

She nodded. Then, very hesitantly: "Those two men—Yost and Funatti—from the Special Investigating Commission? They said no one would be allowed to leave the building."

"Did they now?" he chuckled. "I think they were angry. They've been that way before. But unless and until they can hang something on me—And Ruth, tell my bodyguard to go home, except for the man with the Primeys. He's to check with me, wherever I am, every two hours."

He ambled out, being careful to smile benevolently at every third executive and fifth typist in the large office. A private elevator and entrance was all very well for an occasional crisis, but Hebster liked to taste his successes in as much public as possible.

It would be good to see Kleimbocher again. He had a good deal of faith in the linguistic approach; grants from his corporation had tripled the size of the university's philology department. After all, the basic problem between man and Primey as well as man and Alien was one of communication. Any attempt to learn their science, to adjust their mental processes and logic into safer human channels, would have to be preceded by understanding.

It was up to Kleimbocher to find that understanding, not him. "I'm Hebster," he thought. "I *employ* the people who solve problems. And then I make money off them."

Somebody got in front of him. Somebody else took his arm. "I'm Hebster," he repeated automatically, but out loud. "*Algernon* Hebster."

"Exactly the Hebster we want," Funatti said holding tightly on to his arm. "You don't mind coming along with us?"

"Is this an arrest?" Hebster asked the larger Yost who now moved aside to let him pass. Yost was touching his holstered weapon with dancing fingertips.

The SIC man shrugged. "Why ask such questions?" he

15

countered. "Just come along and be sociable, kind of. People want to talk to you."

He allowed himself to be dragged through the lobby ornate with murals by radical painters and nodded appreciation at the doorman who, staring right through his captors, said enthusiastically, "Good *afternoon*, Mr. Hebster." He made himself fairly comfortable on the back seat of the dark-green SIC car, a late model Hebster Monowheel.

"Surprised to see you minus your bodyguard." Yost, who was driving, remarked over his shoulder.

"Oh, I gave them the day off."

"As soon as you were through with the Primeys? No," Funatti admitted, "we never did find out where you cached them. That's one big building you own, mister. And the UM Special Investigating Commission is notoriously understaffed."

"Not forgetting it's also notoriously underpaid," Yost broke in.

"I couldn't forget that if I tried," Funatti assured him. "You know, Mr. Hebster, I wouldn't have sent my bodyguard off if I'd been in your shoes. Right now there's something about five times as dangerous as Primeys after you. I mean Humanity Firsters."

"Vandermeer Dempsey's crackpots? Thanks, but I think I'll survive."

"That's all right. Just don't give any long odds on the proposition. Those people have been expanding fast and furious. *The Evening Humanitarian* alone has a tremendous circulation. And when you figure their weekly newspapers, their penny booklets and throwaway handbills, it adds up to an impressive amount of propaganda. Day after day they bang away editorially at the people who're making money off the Aliens and Primeys. Of course, they're really hitting at the UM, like always, but if an ordinary Firster met you on the street, he'd be as likely to cut your heart out as not. Not interested? Sorry. Well, maybe you'll like this. *The Evening Humanitarian* has a cute name for you."

Yost guffawed. "Tell him, Funatti."

The corporation president looked at the little man inquiringly.

"They call you," Funatti said with great savoring deliberation, "they call you an interplanetary pimp!"

Emerging at last from the crosstown underpass, they sped up the very latest addition to the strangling city's facilities— the East Side Air-Floating Super-Duper Highway, known familiarly as Dive-Bomber Drive. At the Forty-Second Street offway, the busiest road exit in Manhattan, Yost failed to

16

make a traffic signal. He cursed absent-mindedly and Hebster found himself nodding the involuntary passenger's agreement. They watched the elevator section dwindling downward as the cars that were to mount the highway spiraled up from the right. Between the two, there rose and fell the steady platforms of harbor traffic while, stacked like so many decks of cards, the pedestrian stages awaited their turn below.

"Look! Up there, straight ahead! See it?"

Hebster and Funatti followed Yost's long, waggling forefinger with their eyes. Two hundred feet north of the offway and almost a quarter of a mile straight up, a brown object hung in obvious fascination. Every once in a while a brilliant blue dot would enliven the heavy murk imprisoned in its bell-jar shape only to twirl around the side and be replaced by another.

"Eyes? You think they're eyes?" Funatti asked, rubbing his small dark fists against each other futilely. "I know what the scientists say—that every dot is equivalent to one person and the whole bottle is like a family or a city, maybe. But how do they know? It's a theory, a guess. *I* say they're eyes."

Yost hunched his great body half out of the open window and shaded his vision with his uniform cap against the sun. "Look at it," they heard him say, over his shoulder. A nasal twang, long-buried, came back into his voice as heaving emotion shook out its cultivated accents. "A-setting up there, a-staring and a-staring. So all-fired interested in how we get on and off a busy highway! Won't pay us no never mind when we try to talk to it, when we try to find out what it wants, where it comes from, who it is. Oh, no! It's too superior to talk to the likes of us! But it can watch us, hours on end, days without end, light and dark, winter and summer; it can watch us going about our business; and every time we dumb two-legged animals try to do something *we* find complicated, along comes a blasted 'dots-in-bottle' to watch and sneer and—"

"Hey there, man," Funatti leaned forward and tugged at his partner's green jerkin. "Easy! We're SIC, on business."

"All the same," Yost grunted wistfully, as he plopped back into his seat and pressed the power button, "I wish I had Daddy's little old M-1 Garand right now." They bowled forward, smoothed into the next long elevator section and started to descend. "It would be worth the risk of getting *pinged*."

And this was a UM man, Hebster reflected with acute discomfort. Not only UM, at that, but member of a special group carefully screened for their lack of anti-Primey pre-

17

judice, sworn to enforce the reservation laws without discrimination and dedicated to the proposition that Man could somehow achieve equality with Alien.

Well, how much dirt-eating could people do? People without a business sense, that is. His father had hauled himself out of the pick-and-shovel brigade hand over hand and raised his only son to maneuver always for greater control, to search always for that extra percentage of profit.

But others seemed to have no such abiding interest, Algernon Hebster knew regretfully.

They found it impossible to live with achievements so abruptly made inconsequential by the Aliens. To know with certainty that the most brilliant strokes of which they were capable, the most intricate designs and clever careful workmanship, could be duplicated—and surpassed—in an instant's creation by the outsiders and was of interest to them only as a collector's item. The feeling of inferiority is horrible enough when imagined; but when it isn't feeling but *knowledge*, when it is inescapable and thoroughly demonstrable, covering every aspect of constructive activity, it becomes unbearable and maddening.

No wonder men went berserk under hours of unwinking Alien scrutiny—watching them as they marched in a colorfully uniformed lodge parade, or fished through a hole in the ice, as they painfully maneuvered a giant transcontinental jet to a noiseless landing or sat in sweating, serried rows chanting to a single, sweating man to "knock it out of the park and sew the whole thing up!" No wonder they seized rusty shotgun or gleaming rifle and sped shot after vindictive shot into a sky poisoned by the contemptuous curiosity of a brown, yellow or vermillion "bottle."

Not that it made very much difference. It did give a certain release to nerves backed into horrible psychic corners. But the Aliens didn't notice, and that was most important. The Aliens went right on watching, as if all this shooting and uproar, all these imprecations and weapon-wavings, were all part of the self-same absorbing show they had paid to witness and were determined to see through if for nothing else than the occasional amusing fluff some member of the inexperienced cast might commit.

The Aliens weren't injured, and the Aliens didn't feel attacked. Bullets, shells, buckshot, arrows, pebbles from a slingshot—all Man's miscellany of anger passed through them like the patient and eternal rain coming in the opposite direction. Yet the Aliens had solidity somewhere in their strange

18

bodies. One could judge that by the way they intercepted light and heat. And also—

Also by the occasional *ping*.

Every once in a while, someone would evidently have hurt an Alien slightly. Or more probably just annoyed it by some unknown concomitant of rifle-firing or javelin-throwing.

There would be the barest suspicion of a sound—as if a guitarist had lunged at a string with his fingertip and decided against it one motor impulse too late. And, after this delicate and hardly-heard *ping*, quite unspectacularly, the rifleman would be weaponless. He would be standing there sighting stupidly up along his empty curled fingers, elbow cocked out and shoulder hunched in, like a large oafish child who had forgotten when to end the game. Neither his rifle nor a fragment of it would ever be found. And—gravely, curiously, intently—the Alien would go on watching.

The *ping* seemed to be aimed chiefly at weapons. Thus, occasionally, a 155 mm. howitzer was *pinged*, and also, occasionally, unexpectedly, it might be a muscular arm, curving back with another stone, that would disappear to the accompaniment of a tiny elfin note. And yet sometimes—could it be that the Alien, losing interest, had become careless in its irritation?—the entire man, murderously violent and shrieking, would *ping* and be no more.

It was not as if a counter-weapon were being used, but a thoroughly higher order of reply, such as a slap to an insect bite. Hebster, shivering, recalled the time he had seen a black tubular Alien swirl its amber dots over a new substreet excavation, seemingly entranced by the spectacle of men scrabbling at the earth beneath them.

A red-headed Sequoia of Irish labor had looked up from Manhattan's stubborn granite just long enough to shake the sweat from his eyelids. So doing, he had caught sight of the dot-pulsing observer and paused to snarl and lift his pneumatic drill, rattling it in noisy, if functionless, bravado at the sky. He had hardly been noticed by his mates, when the long, dark, speckled representative of a race beyond the stars turned end over end once and *ping*ed.

The heavy drill remained upright for a moment, then dropped as if it had abruptly realized its master was gone. Gone? Almost, he had never been. So thorough had his disappearance been, so rapid, with so little flicker had he been snuffed out—harming and taking with him nothing else—that it had amounted to an act of gigantic and positive noncreation.

No, Hebster decided, making threatening gestures at the

19

Aliens was suicidal. Worse, like everything else that had been tried to date, it was useless. On the other hand, wasn't the *Humanity First* approach a complete neurosis? What *could* you do?

He reached into his soul for an article of fundamental faith, found it. "I can make money," he quoted to himself. "That's what I'm good for. That's what I can always do."

As they spun to a stop before the dumpy, brown-brick armory that the SIC had appropriated for its own use, he had a shock. Across the street was a small cigar store, the only one on the block. Brand names which had decorated the plate-glass window in all the colors of the copyright had been supplanted recently by great gilt slogans. Familiar slogans they were by now—but this close to a UM office, the Special Investigating Commission itself?

At the top of the window, the proprietor announced his affiliation in two huge words that almost screamed their hatred across the street:

HUMANITY FIRST!

Underneath these, in the exact center of the window, was the large golden initial of the organization, the wedded letters HF arising out of the huge, symbolic safety razor.

And under that, in straggling script, the theme repeated, reworded and sloganized:

"*Humanity first, last and all the time!*"

The upper part of the door began to get nasty:

"*Deport the Aliens! Send them back to wherever they came from!*"

And the bottom of the door made the store-front's only concession to business:

"*Shop here! Shop Humanitarian!*"

"*Humanitarian!*" Funatti nodded bitterly beside Hebster. "Ever see what's left of a Primey if a bunch of Firsters catch him without SIC protection? Just about enough to pick up with a blotter. I don't imagine you're too happy about boycott-shops like that?"

Hebster managed a chuckle as they walked past the saluting, green-uniformed guards. "There aren't very many Primey-inspired gadgets having to do with tobacco. And if there were, one *Shop Humanitarian* outfit isn't going to break me."

But it is, he told himself disconsolately. It is going to break me—if it means what it seems to. Organization membership

20

is one thing and so is planetary patriotism, but business is something else.

Hebster's lips moved slowly, in half-remembered catechism: Whatever the proprietor believes in or does not believe in, he has to make a certain amount of money out of that place if he's going to keep the door free of bailiff stickers. He can't do it if he offends the greater part of his possible clientele.

Therefore, since he's still in business and, from all outward signs, doing quite well, it's obvious that he doesn't have to depend on across-the-street UM personnel. Therefore, there must be a fairly substantial trade to offset this among entirely transient customers who not only don't object to his Firstism but are willing to forego the interesting new gimmicks and lower prices in standard items that Primey technology is giving us.

Therefore, it is entirely possible—from this one extremely random but highly significant sample—that the newspapers I read have been lying and the socio-economists I employ are incompetent. It is entirely possible that the buying public, the only aspect of the public in which I have the slightest interest, is beginning a shift in general viewpoint which will profoundly affect its purchasing orientation.

It is possible that the entire UM economy is now at the top of a long slide into Humanity First domination, the secure zone of fanatic blindness demarcated by men like Vandermeer Dempsey. The highly usurious, commercially speculative economy of Imperial Rome made a similar transition in the much slower historical pace of two millennia ago and became, in three brief centuries, a static unbusinesslike world in which banking was a sin and wealth which had not been inherited was gross and dishonorable.

Meanwhile, people may already have begun to judge manufactured items on the basis of morality instead of usability, Hebster realized, as dim mental notes took their stolid place beside forming conclusions. He remembered a folderful of brilliant explanation Market Research had sent up last week dealing with unexpected consumer resistance to the new Evvakleen dishware. He had dismissed the pages of carefully developed thesis—to the effect that women were unconsciously associating the product's name with a certain Katherine Evvakios who had recently made the front page of every tabloid in the world by dint of some fast work with a breadknife on the throats of her five children and two lovers—with a yawning smile after examining its first brightly colored chart.

"Probably nothing more than normal housewifely suspicion

21

of a radically new idea," he had muttered, "after washing dishes for years, to be told it's no longer necessary! She can't believe her Evvakleen dish is still the same after stripping the outermost film of molecules after a meal. Have to hit that educational angle a bit harder—maybe tie it in with the expendable molecules lost by the skin during a shower."

He'd penciled a few notes on the margin and flipped the whole problem onto the restless lap of Advertising and Promotion.

But then there had been the seasonal slump in furniture—about a month ahead of schedule. The surprising lack of interest in the Hebster Chubbichair, an item which should have revolutionized men's sitting habits.

Abruptly, he could remember almost a dozen unaccountable disturbances in the market recently, and all in consumer goods. That fits, he decided; any change in buying habits wouldn't be reflected in heavy industry for at least a year. The machine tools plants would feel it before the steel mills; the mills before the smelting and refining combines; and the banks and big investment houses would be the last of the dominoes to topple.

With its capital so thoroughly tied up in research and new production, his business wouldn't survive even a temporary shift of this type. Hebster Securities, Inc. could go like a speck of lint being blown off a coat collar.

Which is a long way to travel from a simple little cigar store. Funatti's jitters about growing Firstist sentiment are contagious! he thought.

If only Kleimbocher could crack the communication problem! If we could talk to the Aliens, find some sort of place for ourselves in their universe. The Firsters would be left without a single political leg!

Hebster realized they were in a large, untidy, map-spattered office and that his escort was saluting a huge, even more untidy man who waved their hands down impatiently and nodded them out of the door. He motioned Hebster to a choice of seats. This consisted of several long walnut-stained benches scattered about the room.

P. Braganza, said the desk nameplate with ornate Gothic flow. P. Braganza had a long, twirlable and tremendously thick mustache. Also, P. Braganza needed a haircut badly. It was as if he and everything in the room had been carefully designed to give the maximum affront to Humanity Firsters. Which, considering their crew-cut, closely-shaven, "Cleanliness is next to Manliness" philosophy, meant that there was a lot of gratuitous unpleasantness in this office when a raid on a street demonstration filled it with jostling fanatics, antiseptically clean and dressed with bare-bone simplicity and neatness.

"So you're worrying about Firster effect on business?"

Hebster looked up, startled.

"No, I don't read your mind," Braganza laughed through tobacco-stained teeth. He gestured at the window behind his desk. "I saw you jump just the littlest bit when you noticed that cigar store. And then you stared at it for two full minutes. I knew what you were thinking about."

"Extremely perceptive of you," Hebster remarked dryly.

The SIC official shook his head in a violent negative. "No, it wasn't. It wasn't a bit perceptive. I knew what you were thinking about because I sit up here day after day staring at that cigar store and thinking exactly the same thing. Braganza, I tell myself, that's the end of your job. That's the end of scientific world government. Right there on that cigar-store window."

He glowered at his completely littered desk top for a moment. Hebster's instincts woke up—there was a sales talk in the wind. He realized the man was engaged in the unaccustomed exercise of looking for a conversational gambit. He felt an itch of fear crawl up his intestines. Why should the SIC, whose power was almost above law and certainly above governments, be trying to dicker with him?

Considering his reputation for asking questions with the snarling end of a rubber hose, Braganza was being entirely too gentle, too talkative, too friendly. Hebster felt like a trapped mouse into whose disconcerted ear a cat was beginning to pour complaints about the dog upstairs.

"Hebster, tell me something. What are your goals?"

"I beg your pardon?"

"What do you want out of life? What do you spend your days planning for, your nights dreaming about? Yost likes the girls and wants more of them. Funatti's a family man, five kids. He's happy in his work because his job's fairly secure, and there are all kinds of pensions and insurance policies to back up his life."

Braganza lowered his powerful head and began a slow, reluctant pacing in front of the desk.

"Now, I'm a little different. Not that I mind being a glorified cop. I appreciate the regularity with which the finance office pays my salary, of course; and there are very few women in this town who can say that I have received an offer of affection from them with outright scorn. But the one thing for which I would lay down my life is United Mankind. *Would* lay down my life? In terms of blood pressure and heart strain

23

you might say I've already done it? Braganza, I tell myself, you're a lucky dope. You're working for the first world government in human history. Make it count."

He stopped and spread his arms in front of Hebster. His unbuttoned green jerkin came apart awkwardly and exposed the black slab of hair on his chest. "That's me. That's basically all there is to Braganza. Now if we're to talk sensibly I have to know as much about you. I ask—what are your goals?"

The President of Hebster Securities, Inc., wet his lips. "I am afraid I'm even less complicated."

"That's all right," the other man encouraged. "Put it any way you like."

"You might say that before everything else I am a businessman. I am interested chiefly in becoming a better businessman, which is to say a bigger one. In other words, I want to be richer than I am."

Braganza peered at him intently. "And that's all?"

"All? Haven't you ever heard it said that money isn't everything, but that what it isn't it can buy?"

"It can't buy me."

Hebster examined him coolly. "I don't know if you're a sufficiently desirable commodity. I buy what I need, only occasionally making an exception to please myself."

"I don't like you." Braganza's voice had become thick and ugly. "I never liked your kind and there's no sense being polite. I might as well stop trying. I tell you straight out—I think your guts stink."

Hebster rose. "In that case, I believe I should thank you for—"

"Sit *down!* You were asked here for a reason. I don't see any point to it, but we'll go through the motions. Sit down."

Hebster sat. He wondered idly if Braganza received half the salary he paid Greta Seidenheim. Of course, Greta was talented in many different ways and performed several distinct and separately useful services. No, after tax and pension deductions, Braganza was probably fortunate to receive one third of Greta's salary.

He noticed that a newspaper was being proffered him. He took it. Braganza grunted, clumped back behind his desk and swung his swivel chair around to face the window.

It was a week-old copy of *The Evening Humanitarian*. The paper had lost the "voice-of-a-small-but-highly-articulate-minority" look, Hebster remembered from his last reading of it, and acquired the feel of publishing big business. Even if you cut in half the circulation claimed by the box in the upper

24

left-hand corner, that still gave them three million paying readers.

In the upper right-hand corner, a red-bordered box exhorted the faithful to "*Read Humanitarian!*" A green streamer across the top of the first page announced that "*Making sense is human—to gibber, Prime!*"

But the important item was in the middle of the page. A cartoon.

Half-a-dozen Primeys wearing long, curved beards and insane, tongue-lolling grins, sat in a rickety wagon. They held reins attached to a group of straining and portly gentlemen dressed—somewhat simply—in high silk hats. The fattest and ugliest of these, the one in the lead, had a bit between his teeth. The bit was labeled "*crazy-money*" and the man, "Algernon Hebster."

Crushed and splintering under the wheels of the wagon were such varied items as a "Home Sweet Home" framed motto with a piece of wall attached, a clean-cut youngster in a Boy Scout uniform, a streamlined locomotive and a gorgeous young woman with a squalling infant under each arm.

The caption inquired starkly: "Lords of Creation—Or Serfs?"

"This paper seems to have developed into a fairly filthy scandal sheet," Hebster mused out loud. "I shouldn't be surprised if it makes money."

"I take it then," Braganza asked without turning around from his contemplation of the street, "that you haven't read it very regularly in recent months?"

"I am happy to say I have not."

"That was a mistake."

Hebster stared at the clumped locks of black hair. "Why?" he asked carefully.

"Because it *has* developed into a thoroughly filthy and extremely successful scandal sheet. You're its chief scandal." Braganza laughed. "You see these people look upon Primey dealing as more of a sin than a crime. And, according to that morality, you're close to Old Nick himself!"

Shutting his eyes for a moment, Hebster tried to understand people who imagined such a soul-satisfying and beautiful concept as profit to be a thing of dirt and crawling maggots. He sighed. "I've thought of Firstism as a religion myself."

That seemed to get the SIC man. He swung around excitedly and pointed with both forefingers. "I tell you that you are right! It crosses all boundaries—incompatible and warring creeds are absorbed into it. It is willful, witless denial of

25

a highly painful fact—that there are intellects abroad in the universe which are superior to our own. And the denial grows in strength every day that we are unable to contact the Aliens. If, as seems obvious, there is no respectable place for humanity in this galactic civilization, why, say men like Vandermeer Dempsey, then let us preserve our self-conceit at the least. Let's stay close to and revel in the things that are undeniably human. In a few decades, the entire human race will have been sucked into this blinkered vacuum."

He rose and walked around the desk again. His voice had assumed a terribly earnest, tragically pleading quality. His eyes roved Hebster's face as if searching for a pin-point of weakness, an especially thin spot in the frozen calm.

"Think of it," he asked Hebster. "Periodic slaughters of scientists and artists who, in the judgment of Dempsey, have pushed out too far from the conventional center of so-called humanness. An occasional *auto-da-fé* in honor of a merchant caught selling Primey goods—"

"I shouldn't like that," Hebster admitted, smiling. He thought a moment. "I see the connection you're trying to establish with the cartoon in *The Evening Humanitarian.*"

"Mister, I shouldn't have to. They want your head on the top of a long stick. They want it because you've become a symbol of dealing successfully for your own ends, with these stellar foreigners, or at least their human errand-boys and chambermaids. They figure that maybe they can put a stop to Primey-dealing generally if they put a bloody stop to you. And I tell you this—maybe they are right."

"What exactly do you propose?" Hebster asked in a low voice.

"That you come in with us. We'll make an honest man of you—officially. We want you directing our investigation; except that the goal will not be an extra buck but all-important interracial communication and eventual interstellar negotiation."

The president of Hebster Securities, Inc., gave himself a few minutes on that one. He wanted to work out a careful reply. And he wanted time—above all, he wanted time!

He was so close to a well-integrated and world-wide commercial empire! For ten years, he had been carefully fitting the component industrial kingdoms into place, establishing suzerainty in this production network and squeezing a little more control out of that economic satrapy. He had found delectable tidbits of power in the dissolution of his civilization, endless opportunities for wealth in the shards of his race's self-esteem. He required a bare twelve months now to consolidate and co-ordinate. And suddenly—with the open-mouthed shock of a Jim Fiske who had cornered gold on the Exchange only to have the United States Treasury defeat him by releasing enormous quantities from the Government's own hoard—suddenly, Hebster realized he wasn't going to have the time. He was too experienced a player not to sense that a new factor was coming into the game, something outside his tables of actuarial figures, his market graphs and cargo loading indices.

His mouth was clogged with the heavy nausea of unexpected defeat. He forced himself to answer:

"I'm flattered. Braganza, I *really* am flattered. I see that Dempsey has linked us—we stand or fall together. But—I've always been a loner. With whatever help I can buy, I take care of myself. I'm not interested in any goal but the extra buck. First and last, I'm a businessman."

"Oh, stop it!" the dark man took a turn up and down the office angrily. "This a planet-wide emergency. There are times when you can't be a businessman."

"I deny that. I can't conceive of such a time."

Braganza snorted. "You can't be a businessman if you're strapped to a huge pile of blazing faggots. You can't be a businessman if people's minds are so thoroughly controlled that they'll stop eating at their leader's command. You can't be a businessman, my slavering, acquisitive friend, if demand is so well in hand that it ceases to exist."

"That's impossible!" Hebster had leaped to his feet. To his amazement, he heard his voice climbing up the scale to hysteria. "There's *always* demand. Always! The trick is to find what new form it's taken and then fill it!"

"Sorry! I didn't mean to make fun of your religion."

Hebster drew a deep breath and sat down with infinite care. He could almost feel his red corpuscles simmering.

Take it easy, he warned himself, take it easy! This is a man who must be won, not antagonized. They're changing the rules of the market, Hebster, and you'll need every friend you can buy.

Money won't work with this fellow. But there are *other* values—

"Listen to me, Braganza. We're up against the psycho-social consequences of an extremely advanced civilization hitting a comparatively barbarous one. Are you familiar with Professor Kleimbocher's Firewater Theory?"

"That the Alien's logic hits us mentally in the same way as whisky hit the North American Indian? And the Primeys, representing our finest minds, are the equivalent of those

27

Indians who had the most sympathy with the white man's civilization? Yes. It's a strong analogy. Even carried to the Indians who, lying sodden with liquor in the streets of frontier towns, helped create the illusion of the treacherous, lazy, kill-you-for-a-drink aborigines while being so thoroughly despised by their tribesmen that they didn't dare go home for fear of having their throats cut. I've always felt—"

"The only part of that I want to talk about," Hebster interrupted, "is the firewater concept. Back in the Indian villages, an ever-increasing majority became convinced that firewater and gluttonous paleface civilization were synonymous, that they must rise and retake their land forcibly, killing in the process as many drunken renegades as they came across. This group can be equated with the Humanity Firsters. Then there was a minority who recognized the white men's superiority in numbers and weapons, and desperately tried to find a way of coming to terms with his civilization—terms that would not include his booze. For them read the UM. Finally, there was my kind of Indian."

Braganza knitted voluminous eyebrows and hitched himself up to a corner of the desk. "Hah?" he inquired. "What kind of Indian were *you*, Hebster?"

"The kind who had enough sense to know that the paleface had not the slightest interest in saving him from slow and painful cultural anemia. The kind of Indian, also, whose instincts were sufficiently sound so that he was scared to death of innovations like firewater and wouldn't touch the stuff to save himself from snake bite. But the kind of Indian—"

"Yes?" Go on!"

"The kind who was fascinated by the strange transparent container in which the firewater came! Think how covetous an Indian potter might be of the whisky bottle, something which was completely outside the capacity of his painfully acquired technology. Can't you see him hating, despising and terribly afraid of the smelly amber fluid, which toppled the most stalwart warriors, yet wistful to possess a bottle minus contents? That's about where I see myself, Braganza—the Indian whose greedy curiosity shines through the murk of hysterical clan politics and outsiders' contempt like a lambent flame. I want the new kind of container somehow separated from the firewater."

Unblinkingly, the great dark eyes stared at his face. A hand came up and smoothed each side of the arched mustachio with long, unknowing twirls. Minutes passed.

"Well. Hebster as our civilization's noble savage," the SIC

man chuckled at last, "it almost feels right. But what does it mean in terms of the overall problem?"

"I've told you," Hebster said wearily, hitting the arm of the bench with his open hand, "that I haven't the slightest interest in the overall problem."

"And you only want the bottle. I heard you. But you're not a potter, Hebster—you haven't an elementary particle of craftsman's curiosity. All of that historical romance you spout—you don't care if your world drowns in its own agonized juice. You just want a profit."

"I never claimed an altruistic reason. I leave the general solution to men whose minds are good enough to juggle its complexities—like Kleimbocher."

"Think somebody like Kleimbocher could do it?"

"I'm almost certain he will. That was our mistake from the beginning—trying to break through with historians and psychologists. Either they've become limited by the study of human societies or—well, this is personal, but I've always felt that the science of the mind attracts chiefly those who've already experienced grave psychological difficulty. While they might achieve such an understanding of themselves in the course of their work as to become better adjusted eventually than individuals who had less problems to begin with, I'd still consider them too essentially unstable for such an intrinsically shocking experience as establishing *rapport* with an Alien. Their internal dynamics inevitably make Primeys of them."

Braganza sucked at a tooth and considered the wall behind Hebster. "And all this, you feel, wouldn't apply to Kleimbocher?"

"No, not a philology professor. He has no interest, no intellectual roots in personal and group instability. Kleimbocher's a comparative linguist—a technician, really—a specialist in basic communication. I've been out to the university and watched him work. His approach to the problem is entirely in terms of his subject—communicating with the Aliens instead of trying to understand them. There's been entirely too much intricate speculation about Alien consciousness, sexual attitudes and social organization, about stuff from which we will derive no tangible and immediate good. Kleimbocher's completely pragmatic."

"All right. I follow you. Only he went Prime this morning."

Hebster paused, a sentence dangling from his dropped jaw. "Professor Kleimbocher? *Rudolf* Kleimbocher?" he asked idiotically. "But he was so close . . . he almost had it . . . an elementary signal dictionary . . . he was about to—"

"He *did*. About nine forty-five. He'd been up all night with a Primey one of the psych professors had managed to hypno-

29

tize and gone home unusually optimistic. In the middle of his first class this morning, he interrupted himself in a lecture on medieval cyrillic to . . . to gabble-honk. He sneezed and wheezed at the students for about ten minutes in the usual Primey pattern of initial irritation, then, abruptly giving them up as hopeless, worthless idiots, he levitated himself in that eerie way they almost always do at first. Banged his head against the ceiling and knocked himself out. I don't know what it was, fright, excitement, respect for the old boy perhaps, but the students neglected to tie him up before going for help. By the time they'd come back with the campus SIC man, Kleimbocher had revived and dissolved one wall of the Graduate School to get out. Here's a snapshot of him about five hundred feet in the air, lying on his back with his arms crossed behind his head, skimming west at twenty miles an hour."

The executive studied the little paper rectangle with blinking eyes. "You radioed the air force to chase him, of course."

"What's the use? We've been through *that* enough times. He'd either increase his speed and generate a tornado, drop like a stone and get himself smeared all over the countryside or materialize stuff like wet coffee grounds and gold ingots inside the jets of the pursuing plane. Nobody's caught a Primey yet in the first flush of . . . whatever they do feel at first. And we might stand to lose anything from a fairly expensive hunk of aircraft, including pilot, to a couple of hundred acres of New Jersey topsoil."

Hebster groaned. "But the eighteen years of research that he represented!"

"Yeah. That's where we stand. Blind Alley umpteen hundred thousand or thereabouts. Whatever the figure is, it's awfully close to the end. If you can't crack the Alien on a straight linguistic basis, you can't crack the Alien at all, period, end of paragraph. Our most powerful weapons affect them like bubble pipes, and our finest minds are good for nothing better than to serve them in low, fawning idiocy. But the Primeys are all that's left. We might be able to talk sense to the Man if not the Master."

"Except that Primeys, by definition, don't talk sense."

Braganza nodded. "But since they were human—*ordinary* human—to start with, they represent a hope. We always knew we might some day have to fall back on our only real contact. That's why the Primey protective laws are so rigid; why the Primey reservation compounds surrounding Alien settlements are guarded by our military detachments. The lynch spirit has been evolving into the pogrom spirit as human resentment and discomfort have been growing. Humanity First is beginning to feel strong enough to challenge United Mankind. And honestly, Hebster, at this point neither of us know which would survive a real fight. But you're one of the few who have talked to Primeys, worked with them—"

"Just on business."

"Frankly, that much of a start is a thousand times further along than the best that we've been able to manage. It's so blasted ironical that the only people who've had any conversation at all with the Primeys aren't even slightly interested in the imminent collapse of civilization! Oh, well. The point is that in the present political picture, you sink with us. Recognizing this, my people are prepared to forget a great deal and document you back into respectability. How about it?"

"Funny," Hebster said thoughtfully. "It can't be knowledge that makes miracle-workers out of fairly sober scientists. They all start shooting lightnings at their families and water out of rocks far too early in Primacy to have had time to learn new techniques. It's as if by merely coming close enough to the Aliens to grovel, they immediately move into position to tap a series of cosmic laws more basic than cause and effect."

The SIC man's face slowly deepened into purple. "Well, are you coming in, or aren't you? Remember Hebster, in these times, a man who insists on business as usual is a traitor to history."

"I think Kleimbocher *is* the end," Hebster nodded to himself. "Not much point in chasing Alien mentality if you're going to lose your best men on the way. I say let's forget all this nonsense of trying to live as equals in the same universe with Aliens. Let's concentrate on human problems and be grateful that they don't come into our major population centers and tell us to shove over."

The telephone rang. Braganza had dropped back into his swivel chair. He let the instrument squeeze out several piercing sonic bubbles while he clicked his strong square teeth and maintained a carefully-focused glare at his visitor. Finally, he picked it up, and gave it the verbal minima:

"Speaking. He is here. I'll tell him. 'Bye."

He brought his lips together, kept them pursed for a moment and then, abruptly, swung around to face the window.

"Your office, Hebster. Seems your wife and son are in town and have to see you on business. She the one you divorced ten years ago?"

Hebster nodded at his back and rose once more. "Probably wants her semiannual alimony dividend bonus. I'll have to go. Sonia never does office morale any good."

This meant trouble, he knew. "Wife-and-son" was executive code for something seriously wrong with Hebster Securities, Inc. He had not seen his wife since she had been satisfactorily maneuvered into giving him control of his son's education. As far as he was concerned, she had earned a substantial income for life by providing him with a well-mothered heir.

"Listen!" Braganza said sharply as Hebster reached the door. He still kept his eyes studiously on the street. "I tell you this: You don't want to come in with us. All right! You're a businessman first and a world citizen second. All right! But keep your nose clean, Hebster. If we catch you the slightest bit off base from now on, you'll get hit with everything. We'll not only pull the most spectacular trial this corrupt old planet has ever seen, but somewhere along the line, we'll throw you and your entire organization to the wolves. We'll see to it that *Humanity First* pulls the Hebster Tower down around your ears."

Hebster shook his head, licked his lips. *"Why?* What would that accomplish?"

"Hah! It would give a lot of us here the craziest kind of pleasure. But it would also relieve us temporarily of some of the mass pressure we've been feeling. There's always the chance that Dempsey would lose control of his hotter heads, that they'd go on a real gory rampage, make with the sound and the fury sufficiently to justify full deployment of troops. We could knock off Dempsey and all of the big-shot Firsters then, because John Q. United Mankind would have seen to his own vivid satisfaction and injury what a dangerous mob they are."

"This," Hebster commented bitterly, "is the idealistic, legalistic world government!"

Braganza's chair spun around to face Hebster and his fist came down on the desk top with all the crushing finality of a magisterial gavel. "No, it is not! It is the SIC, a plenipotentiary and highly practical bureau of the UM, especially created to organize a relationship between Alien and human. Furthermore, it's the SIC in a state of the greatest emergency when the reign of law and world government may topple at a demagogue's belch. Do you think"—his head snaked forward belligerently, his eyes slitted to thin lines of purest contempt—"that the career and fortune, even the life, let us say, of as openly selfish a slug as you, Hebster, would be placed above that of the representative body of two billion *socially* operating human beings?"

The SIC official thumped his sloppily buttoned chest. "Braganza, I tell myself now, you're lucky he's too hungry for his

32

blasted profit to take you up on that offer. Think how much fun it's going to be to sink a hook into him when he makes a mistake at last! To drop him onto the back of *Humanity First* so that they'll run amuck and destroy themselves! Oh, get out, Hebster. I'm through with you."

He had made a mistake, Hebster reflected as he walked out of the armory and snapped his fingers at a gyrocab. The SIC was the most powerful single government agency in a Primey-infested world; offending them for a man in his position was equivalent to a cab driver delving into the more uncertain aspects of a traffic cop's ancestry in the policeman's popeyed presence.

But what could he do? Working with the SIC would mean working under Braganza—and since maturity, Algernon Hebster had been quietly careful to take orders from no man. It would mean giving up a business which, with a little more work and a little more time, might somehow still become the dominant combine on the planet. And worst of all, it would mean acquiring a social orientation to replace the calculating businessman's viewpoint which was the closest thing to a soul he had ever known.

The doorman of his building preceded him at a rapid pace down the side corridor that led to his private elevator and flourished aside for him to enter. The car stopped on the twenty-third floor. With a heart that had sunk so deep as to have practically foundered, Hebster picked his way along the wide-eyed clerical stares that lined the corridor. At the entrance to General Laboratory 23B, two tall men in the gray livery of his personal bodyguard moved apart to let him enter. If they had been recalled after having been told to take the day off, it meant that a full-dress emergency was being observed. He hoped that it had been declared in time to prevent any publicity leakage.

It had, Greta Seidenheim assured him. "I was down here applying the clamps five minutes after the fuss began. Floors twenty-one through twenty-five are closed off and all outside lines are being monitored. You can keep your employees an hour at most past five o'clock—which gives you a maximum of two hours and fourteen minutes."

He followed her green-tipped fingernail to the far corner of the lab where a body lay wrapped in murky rags. Theseus. Protruding from his back was the yellowed ivory handle of quite an old German S. S. dagger, 1942 edition. The silver swastika on the hilt had been replaced by an ornate symbol—an HF Blood had soaked Theseus' long matted hair into an ugly red rug.

33

A dead Primey, Hebster thought, staring down hopelessly. In *his* building, in the laboratory to which the Primey had been spirited two or three jumps ahead of Yost and Funatti. This was capital offense material—if the courts ever got a chance to weigh it.

"Look at the dirty Primey-lover!" a slightly familiar voice jeered on his right. "He's scared! Make money out of *that*, Hebster!"

The corporation president strolled over to the thin man with the knobby, completely shaven head who was tied to an unused steampipe. The man's tie, which hung outside his laboratory smock, sported an unusual ornament about halfway down. It took Hebster several seconds to identify it. A miniature gold safety razor upon a black "3."

"He's a third echelon official of *Humanity First!*"

"He's also Charlie Verus of Hebster Laboratories," an extremely short man with a corrugated forehead told him. "My name is Margritt, Mr. Hebster, Dr. J. H. Margritt. I spoke to you on the communicator when the Primeys arrived."

Hebster shook his head determinedly. He waved back the other scientists who were milling around him self-consciously. "How long have third echelon officials, let alone ordinary members of *Humanity First,* been receiving salary checks in my laboratories?"

"I don't know." Margritt shrugged up at him. "Theoretically no Firsters can be Hebster employees. Personnel is supposed to be twice as efficient as the SIC when it comes to sifting background. They probably are. But what can they do when an employee joins *Humanity First* after he passed his probationary period? These proselyting times you'd need a complete force of secret police to keep tabs on all the new converts!"

"When I spoke to you earlier in the day, Margritt, you indicated disapproval of Verus. Don't you think it was your duty to let me know I had a Firster official about to mix it up with Primeys?"

The little man beat a violent negative back and forth with his chin. "I'm paid to supervise research, Mr. Hebster, not to co-ordinate your labor relations nor vote your political ticket!"

Contempt—the contempt of the creative researcher for the businessman-entrepreneur who paid his salary and was now in serious trouble—flickered behind every word he spoke. Why, Hebster wondered irritably, did people so despise a man who made money? Even the Primeys back in his office, Yost and Funatti, Braganza, Margritt—who had worked in his laboratories for years. It was his only talent. Surely, as such, it was as valid as a pianist's?

"I've never liked Charlie Verus," the lab chief went on, "but we never had reason to suspect him of Firstism! He must have hit the third echelon rank about a week ago, eh, Bert?"

"Yeah," Bert agreed from across the room. "The day he came in an hour late, broke every Florence flask in the place and told us all dreamily that one day we might be very proud to tell our grandchildren that we'd worked in the same lab with Charles Bolop Verus."

"Personally," Margritt commented, "I thought he might have just finished writing a book which proved that the Great Pyramid was nothing more than a prophecy in stone of our modern textile designs. Verus was that kind. But it probably was his little safety razor that tossed him up so high. I'd say he got the promotion as a sort of payment in advance for the job he finally did today."

Hebster ground his teeth at the carefully hairless captive who tried, unsuccessfully, to spit in his face; he hurried back to the door where his private secretary was talking to the bodyguard who had been on duty in the lab.

Beyond them, against the wall, stood Larry and S.S. Lusitania conversing in a low-voiced and anxious gabble-honk. They were evidently profoundly disturbed. S. S. Lusitania kept plucking tiny little elephants out of her rags which, kicking and trumpeting tinnily, burst like malformed bubbles as she dropped them on the floor. Larry scratched his tangled beard nervously as he talked, periodically waving a hand at the ceiling which was already studded with fifty or sixty replicas of the dagger buried in Theseus. Hebster couldn't help thinking anxiously of what could have happened to his building if the Primeys had been able to act human enough to defend themselves.

"Listen, Mr. Hebster," the bodyguard began, "I was told not to——"

"Save it," Hebster rapped out. "This wasn't your fault. Even Personnel isn't to blame. Me and my experts deserve to have our necks chopped for falling so far behind the times. We can analyze any trend but the one which will make us superfluous. Greta! I want my roof helicopter ready to fly and my personal stratojet at LaGuardia alerted. Move, girl! And *you* . . . Williams is it?" he queried, leaning forward to read the bodyguard's name on his badge, "Williams, pack these two Primeys into my helicopter upstairs and stand by for a fast take-off."

35

He turned. "Everyone else!" he called. "You will be allowed to go home at six. You will be paid one hour's overtime. Thank you."

Charlie Verus started to sing as Hebster left the lab. By the time he reached the elevator, several of the clerks in the hallway had defiantly picked up the hymn. Hebster paused outside the elevator as he realized that fully one-fourth of the clerical personnel, male and female, were following Verus' cracked and mournful but terribly earnest tenor.

> Mine eyes have seen the coming of
>   the glory of the shorn:
> We will overturn the cess-pool
>   where the Primey slime is born,
> We'll be wearing cleanly garments
>   as we face a human morn—
> The First are on the march!
> Glory, glory, hallelujah,
> Glory, glory, hallelujah . . .

If it was like this in Hebster Securities, he thought wryly as he came into his private office, how fast was *Humanity First* growing among the broad masses of people? Of course, many of those singing could be put down as sympathizers rather than converts, people who were suckers for choral groups and vigilante posses—but how much more momentum did an organization have to generate to acquire the name of political juggernaut?

The only encouraging aspect was the SIC's evident awareness of the danger and the unprecedented steps they were prepared to take as countermeasure.

Unfortunately, the unprecedented steps would take place upon Hebster.

He now had a little less than two hours, he reflected, to squirm out of the most serious single crime on the books of present World Law.

He lifted one of his telephones. "Ruth," he said. "I want to speak to Vandermeer Dempsey. Get me through to him personally."

She did. A few moments later he heard the famous voice, as rich and slow and thick as molten gold. "Hello Hebster, Vandermeer Dempsey speaking." He paused as if to draw breath, then went on sonorously: *"Humanity—may it always be ahead, but, ahead or behind, Humanity!"* He chuckled. "Our newest. What we call our telephone toast. Like it?"

"Very much," Hebster told him respectfully, remember-

36

ing that his former video quizmaster might shortly be church and state combined. "Er . . . Mr. Dempsey, I notice you have a new book out, and I was wondering—"

"Which one? 'Anthropolitics'?"

"That's it. A fine study! You have some very quotable lines in the chapter headed, 'Neither More Nor Less Human.' "

A raucous laugh that still managed to bubble heavily. "Young man, I have quotable lines in every chapter of every book! I maintain a writer's assembly line here at headquarters that is capable of producing up to fifty-five memorable epigrams on any subject upon ten minutes' notice. Not to mention their capacity for political metaphors and two-line jokes with sexy implications! But you wouldn't be calling me to discuss literature, however good a job of emotional engineering I have done in my little text. What is it about, Hebster? Go into your pitch."

"Well," the executive began, vaguely comforted by the Firster chieftain's cynical approach and slightly annoyed at the openness of his contempt, "I had a chat today with your friend and my friend, P. Braganza."

"I know."

"You do? How?"

Vandermeer Dempsey laughed again, the slow, good-natured chortle of a fat man squeezing the curves out of a rocking chair. "Spies, Hebster, *spies*. I have them everywhere practically. This kind of politics is twenty per cent espionge, twenty per cent organization and sixty per cent waiting for the right moment. My spies tell me everything you do."

"They didn't by any chance tell you what Braganza and I discussed?"

"Oh, they did, young man, they did!" Dempsey chuckled a carefree scale exercise. Hebster remembered his pictures: the head like a soft and enormous orange, gouged by a brilliant smile. There was no hair anywhere on the head—all of it, down to the last eyelash and follicled wart, was removed regularly through electrolysis. "According to my agents, Braganza made several strong representations on behalf of the Special Investigating Commission which you rightly spurned. Then, somewhat out of sorts, he announced that if you were henceforth detected in the nefarious enterprises which every one knows have made you one of the wealthiest men on the face of the Earth, he would use you as bait for our anger. I must say I admire the whole ingenious scheme immensely."

"And you're not going to bite," Hebster suggested. Greta Seidenheim entered the office and made a circular gesture at the ceiling. He nodded.

"On the contrary, Hebster, we *are* going to bite. We're going to bite with just a shade more vehemence than we're expected to. We're going to swallow this provocation that the SIC is devising for us and go on to make a world-wide revolution out of it. We *will*, my boy."

Hebster rubbed his left hand back and forth across his lips. "Over my dead body!" He tried to chuckle himself and managed only to clear his throat. "You're right about the conversation with Braganza, and you may be right about how you'll do when it gets down to paving stones and baseball bats. But, if you'd like to have the whole thing a lot easier, there is a little deal I have in mind—"

"Sorry, Hebster my boy. No deals. Not on this. Don't you see we really *don't* want to have it easier? For the same reason, we pay our spies nothing despite the risks they run and the great growing wealth of *Humanity First*. We found that the spies we acquired through conviction worked harder and took many more chances than those forced into our arms by economic pressure. No, we desperately need *L'affaire Hebster* to inflame the populace. We need enough excitement running loose so that it transmits to the gendarmerie and the soldiery, so that conservative citizens who normally shake their heads at a parade will drop their bundles and join the rape and robbery. Enough such citizens and Terra goes *Humanity First*."

"Heads you win, tails I lose."

The liquid gold of Dempsey's laughter poured. "I see what you mean, Hebster. Either way, UM or HF, you wind up a smear-mark on the sands of time. You had your chance when we asked for contributions from public-spirited businessmen four years ago. Quite a few of your competitors were able to see the valid relationship between economics and politics. Woodran of the Underwood Investment Trust is a first echelon official today. Not a single one of *your* top executives wears a razor. But, even so, whatever happens to you will be mild compared to the Primeys."

"The Aliens may object to their body-servants being mauled."

"There are no Aliens!" Dempsey replied in a completely altered voice. He sounded as if he had stiffened too much to be able to move his lips.

"No Aliens? Is that your latest line? You don't mean that!"

"There are only Primeys—creatures who have resigned from human responsibility and are therefore able to do many seemingly miraculous things, which real humanity refuses to do because of the lack of dignity involved. But there are no Aliens. Aliens are a Primey myth."

Hebster grunted. "That is the ideal way of facing an unpleasant fact. Stare right through it."

"If you insist on talking about such illusions as Aliens," the rustling and angry voice cut in, "I'm afraid we can't continue the conversation. You're evidently going Prime, Hebster."

The line went dead.

Hebster scraped a finger inside the mouthpiece rim. "He believes his own stuff!" he said in an awed voice. "For all of the decadent urbanity, he has to have the same reassurance he gives his followers—the horrible, superior thing just isn't there!"

Greta Seidenheim was waiting at the door with his briefcase and both their coats. As he came away from the desk, he said, "I won't tell you not to come along, Greta, but—"

"Good," she said, swinging along behind him. "Think we'll make it to—wherever we're going?"

"Arizona. The first and largest Alien settlement. The place our friends with the funny names come from."

"What can you do there that you can't do here?"

"Frankly, Greta, I don't know. But it's a good idea to lose myself for a while. Then again, I want to get in the area where all this agony originates and take a close look; I'm an off-the-cuff businessman; I've done all of my important figuring on the spot."

There was bad news waiting for them outside the helicopter. "Mr. Hebster," the pilot told him tonelessly while cracking a dry stick of gum, "the stratojet's been seized by the SIC. Are we still going? If we do it in this thing, it won't be very far or very fast."

"We're still going," Hebster said after a moment's hesitation.

They climbed in. The two Primeys sat on the floor in the rear, sneezing conversationally at each other. Williams waved respectfully at his boss. "Gentle as lambs," he said. "In fact, they made one. I had to throw it out."

The large pot-bellied craft climbed up its rope of air and started forward from the Hebster Building.

"There must have been a leak," Greta muttered angrily. "They heard about the dead Primey. Somewhere in the organization there's a leak that I haven't been able to find. The

SIC heard about the dead Primey and now they're hunting us down. Real efficient, I am!"

Hebster smiled at her grimly. She *was* very efficient. So was Personnel and a dozen other subdivisions of the organization. So was Hebster himself. But these were functioning members of a normal business designed for stable times. *Political* spies! If Dempsey could have spies and saboteurs all over Hebster Securities, why couldn't Braganza? They'd catch him before he had even started running; they'd bring him back before he could find a loophole.

They'd bring him back for trial, perhaps, for what in all probability would be known to history as the Bloody Hebster Incident. The incident that had precipitated a world revolution.

"Mr. Hebster, they're getting restless," Williams called out. "Should I relax 'em out, kind off?"

Hebster sat up sharply, hopefully. "No," he said. "Leave them alone!" He watched the suddenly agitated Primeys very closely. This was the odd chance for which he'd brought them along! Years of haggling with Primeys had taught him a lot about them. They were good for other things than sheer gimmick-craft.

Two specks appeared on the windows. They enlarged sleekly into jets with SIC insignia.

"Pilot!" Hebster called, his eyes on Larry who was pulling painfully at his beard. "Get away from the controls! Fast! Did you hear me? That was an *order! Get away from those controls!*"

The man moved off reluctantly. He was barely in time. The control board dissolved into rattling purple shards behind him. The vanes of the gyro seemed to flower into indigo saxophones. Their ears rang with supersonic frequencies as they rose above the jets on a spout of unimaginable force.

Five seconds later they were in Arizona.

They piled out of their weird craft into a sage-cluttered desert.

"I don't ever want to know what my windmill was turned into," the pilot commented, "or what was used to push it along—but how did the Primey come to understand the cops were after us?"

"I don't think he knew that," Hebster explained, "but he was sensitive enough to know he was going home, and that somehow those jets were there to prevent it. And so he functioned, in terms of his interests, in what was almost a human fashion. He protected himself!"

"Going home," Larry said. He'd been listening very closely

to Hebster, dribbling from the right-hand corner of his mouth as he listened. "Haemostat, hammersdarts, hump. Home is where the hate is. Hit is where the hump is. Home and locks the door."

S.S. Lusitania had started on one leg and favored them with her peculiar fleshy smile. "Hindsight," she suggested archly, "is no more than home site. Gabble, honk?"

Larry started after her, some three feet off the ground. He walked the air slowly and painfully as if the road he traveled were covered with numerous small boulders, all of them pitilessly sharp.

"Good-by, people," Hebster said. "I'm off to see the wizard with my friends in greasy gray here. Remember, when the SIC catches up to your unusual vessel—stay close to it for that purpose, by the way—it might be wise to refer to me as someone who forced you into this. You can tell them I've gone into the wilderness looking for a solution, figuring that if I went Prime I'd still be better off than as a punching bag whose ownership is being hotly disputed by such characters as P. Braganza and Vandermeer Dempsey. I'll be back with my mind or on it."

He patted Greta's cheek on the wet spot; then he walked deftly away in pursuit of S.S. Lusitania and Larry. He glanced back once and smiled as he saw them looking curiously forlorn, especially Williams, the chunky young man who earned his living by guarding other people's bodies.

The Primeys followed a route of sorts, but it seemed to have been designed by someone bemused by the motions of an accordion. Again and again it doubled back upon itself, folded across itself, went back a hundred yards and started all over again.

This was Primey country—Arizona, where the first and largest Alien settlement had been made. There were mighty few humans in this corner of the southwest any more—just the Aliens and their coolies.

"Larry," Hebster called as an uncomfortable thought struck him. "Larry! Do . . . do your masters know I'm coming?"

Missing his step as he looked up at Hebster's peremptory question, the Primey tripped and plunged to the ground. He rose, grimaced at Hebster and shook his head. "You are not a businessman," he said. "Here there can be no business. Here there can be only humorous what-you-might-call-worship. The movement to the universal, the inner nature—The realization, complete and eternal, of the partial and evanescent that alone enables . . . that alone enables—" His clawed fingers writhed

41

into each other, as if he were desperately trying to pull a communicable meaning out of the palms. He shook his head with a slow rolling motion from side to side.

Hebster saw with a shock that the old man was crying. Then going Prime had yet another similarity to madness! It gave the human an understanding of something thoroughly beyond himself, a mental summit he was constitutionally incapable of mounting. It gave him a glimpse of some psychological promised land, then buried him, still yearning, in his own inadequacies. And it left him at last bereft of pride in his realizable accomplishments with kind of myopic half-knowledge of where he wanted to go but with no means of getting there.

"When I first came," Larry was saying haltingly, his eyes squinting into Hebster's face, as if he knew what the businessman was thinking, "when first I tried to know . . . I mean the charts and textbooks I carried here, my statistics, my plotted curves were so useless. All playthings I found, disorganized, based on shadow-thought. And then, Hebster, to watch real-thought, real-control! You'll see the joy—You'll serve beside us, you will! Oh, the enormous lifting—"

His voice died into angry incoherencies as he bit into his fist. S.S. Lusitania came up, still hopping on one foot. "Larry," she suggested in a very soft voice, "gabble-honk Hebster away?"

He looked surprised, then noded. The two Primeys linked arms and clambered laboriously back up to the invisible road from which Larry had fallen. They stood facing him for a moment, looking like a weird, ragged, surrealistic version of Tweedledee and Tweedledum.

Then they disappeared and darkness fell around Hebster as if it had been knocked out of the jar. He felt under himself cautiously and sat down on the sand which retained all the heat of daytime Arizona.

Now!

Suppose an Alien came. Suppose an Alien asked him point-blank what it was that he wanted. That would be bad. Algernon Hebster, businessman extraordinary—slightly on the run, at the moment, of course—didn't know what he wanted; not with reference to Aliens.

He didn't want them to leave, because the Primey technology he had used in over a dozen industries was essentially an interpretation and adaptation of Alien methods. He didn't want them to stay because whatever was orderly in his world was dissolving under the acids of their omnipresent superiority.

He also knew that he personally did not want to go Prime.

42

What was left then? Business? Well, there was Braganza's question. What does a businessman do when demand is so well controlled that it can be said to have ceased to exist?

Or what does he do in a case like the present, when demand might be said to be nonexistent, since there was nothing the Aliens seemed to want of Man's puny hoard?

"He *finds* something they want," Hebster said out loud.

How? *How?* Well, the Indian still sold his decorative blankets to the paleface as a way of life, as a source of income. And he insisted on being paid in cash—not firewater. If *only,* Hebster thought, he could somehow contrive to meet an Alien—he'd find out soon enough what its needs were, what was basically desired.

And then as the retort-shaped, the tube-shaped, the bell-shaped bottles materialized all around him, he understood! They had been forming the insistent questions in his mind. And they weren't satisfied with the answers he had found thus far. They liked answers. They liked answers very much indeed. If he was interested, there was always a way—

A great dots-in-bottle brushed his cortex and he screamed. "No! I don't *want* to!" he explained desperately.

Ping! went the dots-in-bottle and Hebster grabbed at his body. His continuing flesh reassured him. He felt very much like the girl in Greek mythology who had begged Zeus for the privilege of seeing him in the full regalia of his godhood. A few moments after her request had been granted, there had been nothing left of the inquisitive female but a fine feathery ash.

The bottles were swirling in and out of each other in a strange and intricate dance from which there radiated emotions vaguely akin to curiosity, yet partaking of amusement and rapture.

Why rapture? Hebster was positive he had caught that note, even allowing for the lack of similarity between mental patterns. He ran a hurried dragnet through his memory, caught a few corresponding items and dropped them after a brief, intensive examination. What was he trying to remember —what was his supremely efficient businessman's instincts trying to remind him of?

The dance became more complex, more rapid. A few bottles had passed under his feet and Hebster could see them, undulating and spinning some ten feet below the surface of the ground as if their presence had made the Earth a transparent as well as permeable medium. Completely unfamiliar with all matters Alien as he was, not knowing—not caring!—whether they danced as an expression of the counsel they were taking together, or as a matter of necessary social ritual,

Hebster was able none the less to sense an approaching climax. Little crooked lines of green lightning began to erupt between the huge bottles. Something exploded near his left ear. He rubbed his face fearfully and moved away. The bottles followed, maintaining him in the imprisoning sphere of their frenzied movements.

Why *rapture?* Back in the city, the Aliens had had a terribly studious air about them as they hovered, almost motionless, above the works and lives of mankind. They were cold and careful scientists and showed not the slightest capacity for . . . for—

So he had something. At last he had something. But what do you do with an idea when you can't communicate it and can't act upon it yourself?

Ping!

The previous invitation was being repeated, more urgently. *Ping! Ping! Ping!*

"No!" he yelled and tried to stand. He found he couldn't. "I'm not . . . I don't want to go Prime!"

There was detached, almost divine laughter.

He felt that awful scrabbling inside his brain as if two or three entities were jostling each other within it. He shut his eyes hard and thought. He was close, he was very close. He had an idea, but he needed time to formulate it—a little while to figure out just exactly what the idea was and just exactly what to do with it!

Ping, ping, ping! Ping, ping, ping!

He had a headache. He felt as if his mind were being sucked out of his head. He tried to hold on to it. He couldn't.

All right, then. He relaxed abruptly, stopped trying to protect himself. But with his mind and his mouth, he yelled. For the first time in his life and with only a partially formed conception of whom he was addressing the desperate call to, Algernon Hebster screamed for help.

"I can do it!" he alternately screamed and thought. "Save money, save time, save whatever it is you want to save, whoever you are and whatever you call yourself—I can help you save! Help me, *help me—We* can do it—but *hurry.* Your problem can be solved—Economize. The balance-sheet—*Help*—"

The words and frantic thoughts spun in and out of each other like the contracting rings of Aliens all around him. He kept screaming, kept the focus on his mental images, while, unbearably, somewhere inside him, a gay and jocular force began to close a valve on his sanity.

Suddenly, he had absolutely no sensation. Suddenly, he knew dozens of things he had never dreamed he could know

44

and had forgotten a thousand times as many. Suddenly, he felt that every nerve in his body was under control of his forefinger. Suddenly, he—

Ping, ping, ping! Ping! Ping! PING! PING! PING! PING!

". . . Like that," someone said.

"What, for example?" someone else asked.

"Well, they don't even lie normally. He's been sleeping like a human being. They twist and moan in their sleep, the Primeys do, for all the world like habitual old drunks. Speaking of moans, here comes our boy."

Hebster sat up on the army cot, rattling his head. The fears were leaving him, and, with the fears gone, he would no longer be hurt. Braganza, highly concerned and unhappy, was standing next to his bed with a man who was obviously a doctor. Hebster smiled at both of them, manfully resisting the temptation to drool out a string of nonsense syllables.

"Hi, fellas," he said. "Here I come, ungathering nuts in May."

"You don't mean to tell me you communicated!" Braganza yelled. "You communicated and didn't go Prime!"

Hebster raised himself on an elbow and glanced out past the tent flap to where Greta Seidenheim stood on the other side of a port-armed guard. He waved his fist at her, and she nodded a wide-open smile back.

"Found me lying in the desert like a waif, did you?"

"*Found* you!" Braganza spat. "You were brought in by Primeys, man. First time in history they ever did that. We've been waiting for you to come to in the serene faith that once you did, everything would be all right."

The corporation president rubbed his forehead. "It will be, Braganza, it will be. Just Primeys, eh? No Aliens helping them?"

"*Aliens?*" Braganza swallowed. "What led you to believe— What gave you reason to hope that . . . that *Aliens* would help the Primeys bring you in?"

"Well, perhaps I shouldn't have used the word 'help.' But I did think there would be a few Aliens in the group that escorted my unconscious body back to you. Sort of an honor guard, Braganza. It would have been a real nice gesture, don't you think?"

The SIC man looked at the doctor who had been following the conversation with interest. "Mind stepping out for a minute?" he suggested.

He walked behind the man and dropped the tent flap into place. Then he came around to the foot of the army cot and pulled on his mustache vigorously. "Now, see here, Hebster, if you keep up this clowning, so help me I will slit your belly

45

open and snap your intestines back in your face! *What happened?*"

"What happened?" Hebster laughed and stretched slowly, carefully, as if he were afraid of breaking the bones of his arm. "I don't think I'll ever be able to answer that question completely. And there's a section of my mind that's very glad that I won't. This much I remember clearly: I had an idea. I communicated it to the proper and interested party. We concluded—this party and I—a tentative agreement as agents, the exact terms of the agreement to be decided by our principals and its complete ratification to be contingent upon their acceptance. Furthermore, we—All right, Braganza, all right! I'll tell it straight. Put down that folding chair. Remember, I've just been through a pretty unsettling experience!"

"Not any worse than the world is about to go through," the official growled. "While you've been out on your three-day vacation, Dempsey's been organizing a full-dress revolution every place at once. He's been very careful to limit it to parades and verbal fireworks so that we haven't been able to make with the riot squads, but it's pretty evident that he's ready to start using muscle. Tomorrow might be it; he's spouting on a world-wide video hookup and it's the opinion of the best experts we have available that his tag line will be the signal for action. Know what their slogan is? It concerns Verus who's been indicted for murder; they claim he'll be a martyr."

"And you were caught with your suspicions down. How many SIC men turned out to be Firsters?"

Braganza nodded. "Not too many, but more than we expected. More than we could afford. He'll do it, Dempsey will, unless you've hit the real thing. Look, Hebster," his heavy voice took on a pleading quality, "don't play with me any more. Don't hold my threats against me; there was no personal animosity in them, just a terrible, fearful worry over the world and its people and the government I was supposed to protect. If you still have a gripe against me, I, Braganza, give you leave to take it out of my hide as soon as we clear this mess up. But let me know where we stand first. A lot of lives and a lot of history depend on what you did out there in that patch of desert."

Hebster told him. He began with the extraterrestrial *Walpurgis Nacht.* "Watching the Aliens slipping in and out of each other in that cock-eyed and complicated rhythm, it struck me how different they were from the thoughtful dots-in-bottles hovering over our busy places, how different all creatures are in their home environments—and how hard it

46

is to get to know them on the basis of their company manners. And then I realized that this place wasn't their home."

"Of course. Did you find out which part of the galaxy they come from?"

"That's not what I mean. Simply because we have marked this area off—and others like it in the Gobi, in the Sahara, in Central Australia—as a reservation for those of our kind whose minds have crumbled under the clear, conscious and certain knowledge of inferiority, we cannot assume that the Aliens around whose settlements they have congregated have necessarily settled themselves."

"*Huh?*" Braganza shook his head rapidly and batted his eyes.

"In other words we had made an assumption on the basis of the Aliens' very evident superiority to ourselves. But that assumption—and therefore that superiority—was in our own terms of what is superior and inferior, and not the Aliens'. And it especially might not apply to those Aliens on . . . the reservation."

The SIC man took a rapid walk around the tent. He beat a great fist into an open sweaty palm. "I'm beginning to, just beginning to—"

"That's what I was doing at that point, just beginning to. Assumptions that don't stand up under the structure they're supposed to support have caused the ruin of more close-thinking businessmen than I would like to face across any conference table. The four brokers, for example, who, after the market crash of 1929—"

"All right," Braganza broke in hurriedly, taking a chair near the cot. "Where did you go from there?"

"I still couldn't be certain of anything; all I had to go on were a few random thoughts inspired by extra-substantial adrenalin secretions and, of course, the strong feeling that these particular Aliens weren't acting the way I had become accustomed to expect Aliens to act. They reminded me of something, of somebody. I was positive that once I got that memory tagged, I'd have most of the problem solved. And I was right."

"How were you right? What was the memory?"

"Well, I hit it backwards, kind of. I went back to Professor Kleimbocher's analogy about the paleface inflicting firewater on the Indian. I've always felt that somewhere in that analogy was the solution. And suddenly, thinking of Professor Kleimbocher and watching those powerful creatures writhing their way in and around each other, suddenly I knew what was wrong. Not the analogy, but our way of using it. We'd picked it up by the hammer head instead of the handle. The paleface gave firewater to the Indian all right—but he got something in return."

"What?"

"Tobacco. Now there's nothing very much wrong with tobacco if it isn't misused, but the first white men to smoke probably went as far overboard as the first Indians to drink. And both booze and tobacco have this in common—they make you awfully sick if you use too much for your initial experiment. See, Braganza? These Aliens out here in the desert reservation are *sick*. They have hit something in our culture that is as psychologically indigestible to them as . . . well, whatever they have that sticks in our mental gullet and causes ulcers among us. They've been put into a kind of isolation in our desert areas until the problem can be licked."

"Something that's as indigestible psychologically—What could it be, Hebster?"

The businessman shrugged irritably. "I don't know. And I don't want to know. Perhaps it's just that they can't let go of a problem until they've solved it—and they can't solve the problems of mankind's activity because of mankind's inherent and basic differences. Simply because we can't understand them, we had no right to assume that they could and did understand us."

"That wasn't all, Hebster. As the comedians put it—everything we can do, they can do better."

"Then why did they keep sending Primeys in to ask for those weird gadgets and impossible gimcracks?"

"They could duplicate anything we made."

"Well, maybe that is it," Hebster suggested. "They could duplicate it, but could they design it? They show every sign of being a race of creatures who never had to make very much for themselves; perhaps they evolved fairly early into animals with direct control over matter, thus never having had to go through the various stages of artifact design. This, in our terms, is a tremendous advantage; but it inevitably would have concurrent disadvantages. Among other things, it would mean a minimum of art forms and a lack of basic engineering knowledge of the artifact itself if not of the directly activated and altered material. The fact is I was right, as I found out later.

For example. Music is not a function of theoretical harmonics, of complete scores in the head of a conductor or composer—these come later, much later. Music is first and foremost a function of the particular instrument, the reed pipe, the skin drum, the human throat—it is a function of tangibles which a race operating upon electrons, positrons and mesons would never encounter in the course of its construction. As

48

soon as I had that, I had the other flaw in the analogy—the assumption itself."

"You mean the assumption that we are necessarily inferior to the Aliens?"

"Right, Braganza. They can do a lot that we can't do, but vice very much indeed versa. How many special racial talents we possess that they don't is a matter of pure conjecture—and may continue to be for a good long time. Let the theoretical boys worry that one a century from now, just so they stay away from it at present."

Braganza fingered a button on his green jerkin and stared over Hebster's head. "No more scientific investigation of them, eh?"

"Well, we can't right now and we have to face up that mildly unpleasant situation. The consolation is that they have to do the same. Don't you see? It's not a basic inadequacy. We don't have enough facts and can't get enough at the moment through normal channels of scientific observation because of the implicit psychological dangers to both races. Science, my forward-looking friend, is a complex of interlocking theories, *all derived from observation.*

"Remember, long before you had any science of navigation you had coast-hugging and river-hopping traders who knew how the various currents affected their leaky little vessels, who had learned things about the relative dependability of the moon and the stars—without any interest at all in integrating these scraps of knowledge into broader theories. Not until you have a sufficiently large body of these scraps, and are able to distinguish the preconceptions from the actual observations, can you proceed to organize a science of navigation without running the grave risk of drowning while you conduct your definitive experiments.

"A trader isn't interested in theories. He's interested only in selling something that glitters for something that glitters even more. In the process, painlessly and imperceptibly, he picks up bits of knowledge which gradually reduce the area of unfamiliarity. Until one day there are enough bits of knowledge on which to base a sort of preliminary understanding, a working hypothesis. And then, some Kleimbocher of the future, operating in an area no longer subject to the sudden and unexplainable mental disaster, can construct meticulous and exact laws out of the more obviously valid hypotheses."

"I might have known it would be something like this, if you came back with it, Hebster! So their theorists and our theorists had better move out and the traders move in. Only how do we contact their traders—if they have any such animals?"

The corporation president sprang out of bed and began dressing. "They have them. Not a Board of Director type perhaps—but a business-minded Alien. As soon as I realized that the dots-in-bottles were acting, relative to their balanced scientific colleagues, very like our own high IQ Primeys, I knew I needed help. I needed someone I could tell about it, someone on their side who had as great a stake in an operating solution as I did. There had to be an Alien in the picture somewhere who was concerned with profit and loss statements, with how much of a return you get out of a given investment of time, personnel, materiel and energy. I figured with him I could talk—*business*. The simple approach: What have you got that we want and how little of what we have will you take for it. No attempts to understand completely incompatible philosophies. There had to be that kind of character somewhere in the expedition. So I shut my eyes and let out what I fondly hoped was a telepathic *yip* channeled to him. I was successful.

"Of course, I might not have been successful if he hadn't been searching desperately for just that sort of *yip*. He came buzzing up in a rousing United States Cavalry-routs-the-redskins type of rescue, stuffed my dripping psyche back into my subconscious and hauled me up into some sort of never-never-ship. I've been in this interstellar version of Mohammed's coffin, suspended between Heaven and Earth, for three days, while he alternately bargained with me and consulted the home office about developments.

"We dickered the way I do with Primeys—by running down a list of what each of us could offer and comparing it with what we wanted; each of us trying to get a little more than we gave to the other guy, in our own terms, of course. Buying and selling are intrinsically simple processes; I don't imagine our discussions were very much different from those between a couple of Phoenician sailors and the blue-painted Celtic inhabitants of early Britain."

"And this . . . this business-Alien never suggested the possibility of taking what they wanted—"

"By force? No, Braganza, not once. Might be they're too civilized for such shenanigans. Personally, I think the big reason is that they don't have any idea of what it is they do want from us. We represent a fantastic enigma to them—a species which uses matter to alter matter, producing objects which, while intended for similar functions, differ enormously from each other. You might say that we ask the question '*how?*' about their activities; and they want to know the '*why?*' about ours. Their investigators have compulsions even greater than ours. As I understand it, the intelligent races they've encountered up to this point are all comprehensible to them since they derive from parallel evolutionary paths. Every time one of their researchers get close to the answer of why we wear various colored clothes even in climates where clothing is unnecessary, he slips over the edges and splashes.

"Of course, that's why this opposite number of mine was so worried. I don't know his exact status—he may be anything from the bookkeeper to the business-manager of the expedition—but it's his bottle-neck if the outfit continues to be uneconomic. And I gathered that not only has his occupation kind of barred him from doing the investigation his unstable pals were limping back from into the asylums he's constructed here in the deserts, but those of them who've managed to retain their sanity constantly exhibit a healthy contempt for him. They feel, you see, that their function is that of the expedition. He's strictly supercargo. Do you think it bothers them one bit," Hebster snorted, "that he has a report to prepare, to show how his expedition stood up in terms of a balance sheet—"

"Well, you did manage to communicate on that point, at least," Braganza grinned. "Maybe traders using the simple, earnestly chiseling approach will be the answer. You've certainly supplied us with more basic data already than years of heavily subsidized research. Hebster I want you to go on the air with this story you told me and show a couple of Primey Aliens to the video public."

"Uh-uh. You tell 'em. You can use the prestige. I'll think a message to my Alien buddy along the private channel he's keeping open for me, and he'll send you a couple of human-happy dots-in-bottles for the telecast. I've got to whip back to New York and get my entire outfit to work on a really encyclopedic job."

"Encyclopedic?"

The execuve pulled his belt tight and reached for a tie. "Well, what else would you call the first edition of the Hebster Interstellar Catalogue of all Human Activity and Available Artifacts, prices available upon request with the understanding that they are subject to change without notice?"

Time in Advance

Twenty minutes after the convict ship landed at the New York Spaceport, reporters were allowed aboard. They came boiling up the main corridor, pushing against the heavily armed guards who were conducting them, the feature-story men and by-line columnists in the lead, the TV people with their portable but still-heavy equipment cursing along behind.

As they went, they passed little groups of spacemen in the black-and-red uniform of the Interstellar Prison Service walking rapidly in the opposite direction, on their way to enjoy five days of planetside leave before the ship roared away once more with a new cargo of convicts.

The impatient journalists barely glanced at these drab personalities who were spending their lives in a continuous shuttle from one end of the Galaxy to the other. After all, the life and adventures of an IPS man had been done thousands of times, done to death. The big story lay ahead.

In the very belly of the ship, the guards slid apart two enormous sliding doors—and quickly stepped aside to avoid being trampled. The reporters almost flung themselves against the iron bars that ran from floor to ceiling and completely shut off the great prison chamber. Their eager, darting stares were met with at most a few curious glances from the men in coarse gray suits who lay or sat in the tiers of bunks that rose in row after sternly functional row all the way down the cargo hold. Each man clutched—and some caressed—a small package neatly wrapped in plain brown paper.

The chief guard ambled up on the other side of the bars, picking the morning's breakfast out of his front teeth. "Hi, boys," he said. "Who're you looking for—as if I didn't know?"

One of the older, more famous columnists held the palm of his hand up warningly. "Look, Anderson: no games. The ship's been almost a half-hour late in landing and we were stalled for fifteen minutes at the gangplank. Now where the hell are they?"

Anderson watched the TV crews shoulder a place for themselves and their equipment right up to the barrier. He tugged a last bit of food out of one of his molars.

"Ghouls," he muttered. "A bunch of grave-happy, funeral-hungry ghouls." Then he hefted his club experimentally a couple of times and clattered it back and forth against the bars. "Crandall!" he bellowed. "Henck! Front and center!"

The cry was picked up by the guards strolling about, steadily, measuredly, club-twirlingly, inside the prison pen. "Crandall! Henck! Front and center!" It went ricocheting authoritatively up and down the tremendous curved walls. "Crandall! Henck! Front and center!"

Nicholas Crandall sat up cross-legged in his bunk on the fifth tier and grimaced. He had been dozing and now he rubbed a hand across his eyes to erase the sleep. There were three parallel scars across the back of his hand, old and brown and straight scars such as an animal's claws might rake out. There was also a curious zigzag scar just above his eyes that had a more reddish novelty. And there was a tiny, perfectly round hole in the middle of his left ear which, after coming fully awake, he scratched in annoyance.

"Reception committee," he grumbled. "Might have known. Same old goddam Earth as ever."

He flipped over on his stomach and reached down to pat the face of the little man snoring on the bunk immediately under him. "Otto," he called. "Blotto Otto—up and at 'em! They want us."

Henck immediately sat up in the same cross-legged fashion, even before his eyes had opened. His right hand went to his throat where there was a little network of zigzag scars of the same color and size as the one Crandall had on his forehead. The hand was missing an index and forefinger.

"Henck here, sir," he said thickly, then shook his head and stared up at Crandall. "Oh—Nick. What's up?"

"We've arrived, Blotto Otto," the taller man said from the bunk above. "We're on Earth and they're getting our discharges ready. In about half an hour, you'll be able to wrap that tongue of yours around as much brandy, beer, vodka and rotgut whiskey as you can pay for. No more prison-brew, no more raisin-jack from a tin can under the bed, Blotto Otto."

Henck grunted and flopped down on his back again. "In half an hour, but not now, so why did you have to go and wake me up? What do you take me for, some dewy, post-crime, petty-larceny kid, sweating out my discharge with my eyes open and my gut wriggling? Hey, Nick, I was dreaming of a new way to get Elsa, a brand-new, really ugly way."

"The screws are in an uproar," Crandall told him, still in a low, patient voice. "Hear them? They want us, you and me."

Henck sat up again, listened a moment, and nodded. "Why is it," he asked, "that only space-screws have voices like that?"

"It's a requirement of the service," Crandall assured him. "You've got to be at least a minimum height, have a minimum education and with a minimum nasty voice of just the right ear-splitting quality before you can get to be a space-screw. Otherwise, no matter how vicious a personality you have, you are just plain out of luck and have to stay behind on Earth and go on getting your kicks by running down slowpoke 'copters driven by old ladies."

A guard stopped below, banged angrily at one of the metal posts that supported their tier of bunks. "Crandall! Henck! You're still convicts, don't you forget that! If you don't front-and-center in a double-time hurry, I'll climb up there and work you over once more for old-time's sake!"

"Yes, *sir*! Coming, *sir*!" they said in immediate, mumbling unison and began climbing down from bunk to bunk, each still clutching the brown-paper package that contained the clothes they had once worn as free men and would shortly be allowed to wear again.

"Listen, Otto." Crandall leaned down as they climbed and brought his lips close to the little man's ear in the rapid-fire, extremely low-pitched prison whisper. "They're taking us to meet the television and news boys. We're going to be asked a lot of questions. One thing you want to be sure to keep your lip buttoned about——"

"Television and news? Why us? What do they want with us?"

"Because we're celebrities, knockhead! We've seen it through for the big rap and come out on the other side. How many men do you think have made it? But *listen*, will you? If they ask you who it is you're after, you just shut up and smile. You don't answer that question. Got that? You don't tell them whose murder you were sentenced for, no matter what they say. They can't make you. That's the law."

Henck paused a moment, one and a half bunks from the floor. "But, Nick, *Elsa* knows! I told her that day, just before I turned myself in. She knows I wouldn't take a murder rap for anyone but her!"

"She knows, she knows, of *course* she knows!" Crandall swore briefly and almost inaudibly. "But she can't *prove* it, you goddam human blotter! Once you say so in public, though, she's entitled to arm herself and shoot you down on sight—pleading self-defense. And till you say so, she can't; she's still your poor wife whom you've promised to love, honor and cherish. As far as the world is concerned——"

The guard reached up with his club and jolted them both angrily across the back. They dropped to the floor and cringed as he snarled over them: "Did I say you could have a talk-party? *Did I?* If we have any time left before you get your discharge, I'm taking you cuties into the guard-room for one last big going-over. Now pick them up and put them down!"

They scuttled in front of him obediently, like a pair of chickens before a snapping collie. At the barred gate near the end of the prison hold, he saluted and said: "Pre-criminals Nicholas Crandall and Otto Henck, sir."

Chief Guard Anderson wiped the salute back at him carelessly. "These gentlemen want to ask you fellas a couple of questions. Won't hurt you to answer. That's all, O'Brien."

His voice was very jovial. He was wearing a big, gentle, half-moon smile. As the subordinate guard saluted and moved away, Crandall let his mind regurgitate memories of Anderson all through this month-long trip from Proxima Centaurus. Anderson nodding thoughtfully as that poor Minelli—Steve Minelli, hadn't that been his name?—was made to run through a gauntlet of club-swinging guards for going to the toilet without permission. Anderson chuckling just a moment before he'd kicked a gray-headed convict in the groin for talking on the chow-line. Anderson—

Well, the guy had guts, anyway, knowing that his ship carried two pre-criminals who had served out a murder sentence. But he probably also knew that they wouldn't waste the murder on him, however viciously he acted. A man doesn't volunteer for a hitch in hell just so he can knock off one of the devils.

"Do we have to answer these questions, sir?" Crandall asked cautiously, tentatively.

The chief guard's smile lost the tiniest bit of its curvature. "I said it wouldn't hurt you, didn't I? But other things might. They *still* might, Crandall. I'd like to do these gentlemen from the press a favor, so you be nice and cooperative, eh?" He gestured with his chin, ever so slightly, in the direction of the guard-room and hefted his club a bit.

"Yes, sir," Crandall said, while Henck nodded violently. "We'll be cooperative, sir."

Dammit, he thought, *if only I didn't have such a use for that murder! Let's keep remembering Stephanson, boy, no one but Stephanson! Not Anderson, not O'Brien, not anybody else: the name under discussion is Frederick Stoddard Stephanson!*

While the television men on the other side of the bars were fussing their equipment into position, the two convicts

55

answered the preliminary, inevitable questions of the feature writers:

"How does it feel to be back?"

"Fine, just fine."

"What's the first thing you're going to do when you get your discharge?"

"Eat a good meal." (From Crandall.)

"Get roaring drunk." (From Henck.)

"Careful you don't wind up right behind bars again as a post-criminal." (From one of the feature writers.) A good-natured laugh in which all of them, the newsmen, Chief Guard Anderson, and Crandall and Henck, participated.

"How were you treated while you were prisoners?"

"Oh, pretty good." (From both of them, concurrent with a thoughtful glance at Anderson's club.)

"Either of you care to tell us who you're going to murder?"

(Silence.)

"Either of you changed your mind and decided not to commit the murder?"

(Crandall looked thoughtfully up, while Henck looked thoughtfully down.) Another general laugh, a bit more uneasy this time, Crandall and Henck not participating.

"All right, we're set. Look this way, please," the television announcer broke in. "And smile, men—let's have a really *big* smile."

Crandall and Henck dutifully emitted big smiles, which made three smiles, for Anderson had moved into the cheerful little group.

The two cameras shot out of the grasp of their technicians, one hovering over them, one moving restlessly before their faces, both controlled, at a distance, by the little box of switches in the cameramen's hands. A red bulb in the nose of one of the cameras lit up.

"Here we are, ladies and gentlemen of the television audience," the announcer exuded in a lavish voice. "We are on board the convict ship *Jean Valjean*, which has just landed at the New York Spaceport. We are here to meet two men—two of the rare men who have managed to serve all of a voluntary sentence for murder and thus are legally entitled to commit one murder apiece.

"In just a few moments, they will be discharged after having served out seven full years on the convict planets—and they will be free to kill any man or woman in the Solar System with absolutely no fear of any kind of retribution. Take a good look at them, ladies and gentlemen of the television audience—it might be you they are after!"

After this cheering thought, the announcer let a moment or two elapse while the cameras let their lenses stare at the two men in prison gray. Then he stepped into range himself and addressed the smaller man.

"What is your name, sir?" he asked.

"Pre-criminal Otto Henck, 525514," Blotto Otto responded automatically, though not able to repress a bit of a start at the *sir*.

"How does it feel to be back?"

"Fine, just fine."

"What's the first thing you're going to do when you get your discharge?"

Henck hesitated, then said, "Eat a good meal," after a shy look at Crandall.

"How were you treated while you were a prisoner?"

"Oh, pretty good. As good as you could expect."

"As good as a criminal could expect, eh? Although you're not really a criminal yet, are you? You're a pre-criminal."

Henck smiled as if this were the first time he was hearing the term. "That's right, sir. I'm a pre-criminal."

"Want to tell the audience who the person is you're going to become a criminal for?"

Henck looked reproachfully at the announcer, who chuckled throatily—and alone.

"Or if you've changed your mind about him or her?" There was a pause. Then the announcer said a little nervously: "You've served seven years on danger-filled, alien planets, preparing them for human colonization. That's the maximum sentence the law allows, isn't it?"

"That's right, sir. With the pre-criminal discount for serving the sentence in advance, seven years is the most you can get for murder."

"Bet you're glad we're not back in the days of capital punishment, eh? That would make the whole thing impractical, wouldn't it? Now, Mr. Henck—or pre-criminal Henck, I guess I should still call you—suppose you tell the ladies and gentlemen of our television audience: What was the most horrifying experience you had while you were serving your sentence?"

"Well," Otto Henck considered carefully. "About the worst of the lot, I guess, was the time on Antares VIII, the second prison camp I was in, when the big wasps started to spawn. They got a wasp on Antares VIII, see, that's about a hundred times the size of—"

"Is that how you lost two fingers on your right hand?"

Henck brought his hand up and studied it for a moment. "No. The forefinger—I lost the forefinger on Rigel XII. We

57

were building the first prison camp on the planet and I dug up a funny kind of red rock that had all sorts of little bumps on it. I poked it, kind of—you know, just to see how hard it was or something—and the tip of my finger disappeared. *Pow*— just like that. Later on, the whole finger got infected and the medics had to cut it off.

"It turned out I was lucky, though; some of the men—the convicts, I mean—ran into bigger rocks than the one I found. Those guys lost arms, legs—one guy even got swallowed whole. They weren't really rocks, see. They were alive—they were alive and hungry! Rigel XII was lousy with them. The middle finger—I lost the middle finger in a dumb kind of accident on board ship while we were being moved to—"

The announcer nodded intelligently, cleared his throat and said: "But those wasps, those giant wasps on Antares VIII— they were the worst?"

Blotto Otto blinked at him for a moment before he found the conversation again.

"Oh. They sure were! They were used to laying their eggs in a kind of monkey they have on Antares VIII, see? It was real rough on the monkey, but that's how the baby wasps got their food while they were growing up. Well, we get out there and it turns out that the wasps can't see any difference between those Antares monkeys and human beings. First thing you know, guys start collapsing all over the place and when they're taken to the dispensary for an X-ray, the medics see that they're completely crammed—"

"Thank you very much, Mr. Henck, but Herkimer's Wasp has already been seen by and described to our audience at least three times in the past on the Interstellar Travelogue, which is carried by this network, as you ladies and gentlemen no doubt remember, on Wednesday evening from seven to seven-thirty P.M. terrestrial standard time. And now, Mr. Crandall, let me ask you, sir: How does it feel to be back?"

Crandall stepped up and was put through almost exactly the same verbal paces as his fellow prisoner.

There was one major difference. The announcer asked him if he expected to find Earth much changed. Crandall started to shrug, then abruptly relaxed and grinned. He was careful to make the grin an extremely wide one, exposing a maximum of tooth and a minimum of mirth.

"There's one big change I can see already," he said. "The way those cameras float around and are controlled from a little switch-box in the cameraman's hand. That gimmick wasn't around the day I left. Whoever invented it must have been pretty clever."

"Oh, yes?" The announcer glanced briefly backward. "You mean the Stephanson Remote Control Switch? It was invented by Frederick Stoddard Stephanson about five years ago—Was it five years, Don?"

"Six years," said the cameraman. "Went on the market five years ago."

"It was *invented* six years ago," the announcer translated. "It went on the market *five* years ago."

Crandall nodded. "Well, this Frederick Stoddard Stephanson must be a clever man, a very clever man." And he grinned again into the cameras. *Look at my teeth,* he thought to himself. *I know you're watching, Freddy. Look at my teeth and shiver.*

The announcer seemed a bit disconcerted. "Yes," he said. "Exactly. Now, Mr. Crandall, what would you describe as the most horrifying experience in your entire . . ."

After the TV men had rolled up their equipment and departed, the two pre-criminals were subjected to a final barrage of questions from the feature writers and columnists in search of odd shreds of color.

"What about the women in your life?" "What books, what hobbies, what amusements filled your time?" "Did you find out that there are no atheists on convict planets?" "If you had the whole thing to do over again—"

As he answered, drably, courteously, Nicholas Crandall was thinking about Frederick Stoddard Stephanson seated in front of his luxurious wall-size television set.

Would Stephanson have clicked it off by now? Would he be sitting there, staring at the blank screen, pondering the plans of the man who had outlived odds estimated at ten thousand to one and returned after seven full, unbelievable years in the prison camps of four insane planets?

Would Stephanson be examining his blaster with sucked-in lips—the blaster that he might use only in an open-and-shut situation of self-defense? Otherwise, he would incur the full post-criminal sentence for murder, which, without the fifty per cent discount for punishment voluntarily undergone in advance of the crime, was as much as fourteen years in the many-pronged hell from which Crandall had just returned?

Or would Stephanson be sitting, slumped in an expensive bubblechair, glumly watching a still-active screen, frightened out of his wits but still unable to tear himself away from the well-organized program the network had no doubt built around the return of two—count 'em: *two!*—homicidal pre-criminals?

At the moment, in all probability, the screen was showing

an interview with some Earthside official of the Interstellar Prison Service, an expansive public relations character who had learned to talk in sociology.

"Tell me, Mr. Public Relations," the announcer would ask (a different announcer, more serious, more intellectual), "how often do pre-criminals serve out a sentence for murder and return?"

"According to statistics—" a rustle of papers at this point and a penetrating glance downward—"according to statistics, we may expect a man who has served a full sentence for murder, with the 50 per cent pre-criminal discount, to return only once in 11.7 years on the average."

"You would say, then, wouldn't you, Mr. Public Relations, that the return of two such men on the same day is a rather unusual situation?"

"*Highly* unusual or you television fellas wouldn't be in such a fuss over it." A thick chuckle here, which the announcer dutifully echoes.

"And what, Mr. Public Relations, happens to the others who don't return?"

A large, well-fed hand gestures urbanely. "They get killed. Or they give up. Those are the only two alternatives. Seven years is a long time to spend on those convict planets. The work schedule isn't for sissies and neither are the life-forms they encounter—the big man-eating ones as well as the small virus-sized types.

"That's why prison guards get such high salaries and such long leaves. In a sense, you know, we haven't really abolished capital punishment; we've substituted a socially useful form of Russian Roulette for it. Any man who commits or pre-commits one of a group of particularly reprehensible crimes is sent off to a planet where his services will benefit humanity and where he's forced to take his chances on coming back in one piece, if at all. The more serious the crime, the longer the sentence and, therefore, the more remote the chances."

"I see. Now, Mr. Public Relations, you say they either get killed or they give up. Would you explain to the audience, if you please, just how they give up and what happens if they do?"

Here a sitting back in the chair, a locking of pudgy fingers over paunch. "You see, any pre-criminal may apply to his warden for immediate abrogation of sentence. It's just a matter of filling out the necessary forms. He's pulled off work detail right then and there and is sent home on the very next ship out of the place. The catch is this: Every bit of time he's served up to that point is canceled—he gets nothing for it.

60

"If he commits an actual crime after being freed, he has to serve the full sentence. If he wants to be committed as a pre-criminal again, he has to start serving the sentence, with the discount, from the beginning. Three out of every four pre-criminals apply for abrogation of sentence in their very first year. You get a bellyful fast in those places."

"I guess you certainly do," agrees the announcer. "What about the discount, Mr. Public Relations? Aren't there people who feel that's offering the pre-criminal too much inducement?"

The barest grimace of anger flows across the sleek face, to be succeeded by a warm, contemptuous smile. "Those are people, I'm afraid, who, however well-intentioned, are not well versed in the facts of modern criminology and penology. We don't want to discourage pre-criminals; we want to *encourage* them to turn themselves in.

"Remember what I said about three out of four applying for abrogation of sentence in their very first year? Now these are individuals who were sensible enough to try to get a discount on their sentence. Are they likely to be foolish enough to risk twice as much when they have found out conclusively they can't stand a bare twelve months of it? Not to mention what they have discovered about the value of human life, the necessity for social cooperation and the general desirability of civilized processes on those worlds where simple survival is practically a matter of a sweepstakes ticket.

"The man who doesn't apply for abrogation of sentence? Well, he has that much more time to let the desire to commit the crime go cold—and that much greater likelihood of getting killed with nothing to show for it. Therefore, so few pre-criminals In *any* of the categories return to tell the tale and do the deed that the social profit is absolutely enormous! Let me give you a few figures.

"Using the Lazarus Scale, it has been estimated that the decline in premeditated homicides alone, since the institution of the pre-criminal discount, has been forty-one per cent on Earth, thirty-three and a third per cent on Venus, twenty-seven per cent—"

Cold comfort, chillingly cold comfort, that would be to Stephanson, Nicholas Crandall reflected pleasurably, those forty-one per cents and thirty-three and a third per cents. Crandall's was the balancing statistic: the man who wanted to murder, and for good and sufficient cause, one Frederick Stoddard Stephanson. He was a leftover fraction on a page of reductions and cancellations—he had returned, astonishingly, unbelievably, after seven years to collect the merchandise for which he had paid in advance.

61

He and Henck. Two ridiculously long long-shots. Henck's wife Elsa—was she, too, sitting in a kind of bird-hypnotized-by-a-snake fashion before her television set, hoping dimly and desperately that some comment of the Interstellar Prison Service official would show her how to evade her fate, how to get out from under the ridiculously rare disaster that was about to happen to her?

Well, Elsa was Blotto Otto's affair. Let him enjoy it in his own way; he'd paid enough for the privilege. But Stephanson was Crandall's.

Oh, let the arrogant bean-pole sweat, he prayed. *Let me take my time and let him sweat!*

The newsman kept squeezing them for story angles until a loudspeaker in the overhead suddenly cleared its diaphragm and announced:

"Prisoners, prepare for discharge! You will proceed to the ship warden's office in groups of ten, as your name is called. Convict ship discipline will be maintained throughout. Arthur, Augluk, Crandall, Ferrara, Fu-Yen, Garfinkel, Gomez, Graham, Henck—"

A half hour later, they were walking down the main corridor of the ship in their civilian clothes. They showed their discharges to the guard at the gangplank, smiled still cringingly back at Anderson, who called from a porthole, "Hey, fellas, come back soon!" and trotted down the incline to the surface of a planet they had not seen for seven agonizing and horror-crowded years.

There were a few reporters and photographers still waiting for them, and one TV crew which had been left behind to let the world see how they looked at the moment of freedom.

Questions, more questions to answer, which they could afford to be brusque about, although brusqueness to any but fellow prisoners still came hard.

Fortunately, the newsmen got interested in another pre-criminal who was with them. Fu-Yen had completed the discounted sentence of two years for aggravated assault and battery. He had also lost both arms and one leg to a corrosive moss on Procyon III just before the end of his term and came limping down the gangplank on one real and one artificial leg, unable to grasp the hand-rails.

As he was being asked, with a good deal of interest, just how he intended to commit simple assault and battery, let alone the serious kind, with his present limited resources, Crandall nudged Henck and they climbed quickly into one of the many hovering gyrocabs. They told the driver to take them to a bar—any quiet bar—in the city.

Blotto Otto almost went to pieces under the impact of actual free choice. "I can't do it," he whispered. "Nick, there's just too damn much to drink!"

Crandall settled it by ordering for him. "Two double scotches," he told the waitress. "Nothing else."

When the scotch came, Blotto Otto stared at it with the kind of affectionate and wistful astonishment a man might show toward an adolescent son whom he saw last as a babe in arms. He put out a gingerly, trembling hand.

"Here's death to our enemies," Crandall said, and tossed his down. He watched Otto sip slowly and carefully, tasting each individual drop.

"You'd better take it easy," he warned. "Elsa might have no more trouble from you than bringing flowers every visiting day to the alcoholic ward."

"No fear," Blotto Otto growled into his empty glass. "I was weaned on this stuff. And, anyway, it's the last drink I have until I dump her. That's the way I've been figuring it, Nick: one drink to celebrate, then Elsa. I didn't go through those seven years to mess myself up at the payoff."

He set the glass down. "Seven years in one steaming hell after another. And before that, twelve years with Elsa. Twelve years with her pulling every dirty trick in the book on me, laughing in my face, telling me she was my wife and had me legally where she wanted me, that I was gonna support her the way she wanted to be supported and I was gonna like it. And if I dared to get off my knees and stand on my hind legs, *pow*, she found a way to get me arrested.

"The weeks I spent in the cooler, in the workhouse, until Elsa would tell the judge maybe I'd learned my lesson, she was willing to give me one more chance! And me begging for a divorce on my knees—hell, on my belly!—no children, she's able-bodied, she's young, and her laughing in my face. When she wanted me in the cooler, see, then she's crying in front of the judge; but when we're alone, she's always laughing her head off to see me squirm.

"I supported her, Nick. Honest, I gave her almost every cent I made, but that wasn't enough. She liked to see me squirm; she *told* me she did. Well, who's squirming now?" He grunted deep in his throat. "Marriage—it's for chumps!"

Crandall looked out of the open window he was sitting against, down through the dizzy, busy levels of Metropolitan New York.

"Maybe it is," he said thoughtfully. "I wouldn't know. My marriage was good while it lasted, five years of it. Then, all of a sudden, it wasn't good any more, just so much rancid butter."

"At least she gave you a divorce," said Henck. "She didn't take you."

"Oh, Polly wasn't the kind of girl to take anyone. A little mixed up, but maybe no more than I was. Pretty Polly, I called her; Big Nick, she called me. The starlight faded and so did I, I guess. I was still knocking myself out then trying to make a go out of the wholesale electronics business with Irv. Anyone could tell I wasn't cut out to be a millionaire. Maybe that was it. Anyway, Polly wanted out and I gave it to her. We parted friends. I wonder, every once in a while, what she's—"

There was a slight splashy noise, like a seal's flipper making a gesture in the water. Crandall's eyes came back to the table a moment after the green, melonlike ball had hit it. And, at the same instant, Henck's hand had swept the ball up and hurled it through the window. The long, green threads streamed out of the ball, but by then it was falling down the side of the enormous building and the threads found no living flesh to take root in.

From the corner of his eye, Crandall had seen a man bolt out of the bar. By the way people kept looking back and forth fearfully from their table to the open doorway, he deduced that the man had thrown it. Evidently Stephanson had thought it worthwhile to have Crandall followed and neutralized.

Blotto Otto saw no point in preening over his reflexes. The two of them had learned to move fast a long time ago—over a lot of dead bodies. "A Venusian dandelion bomb," he observed. "Well, at least the guy doesn't want to kill you, Nick. He just wants to cripple you."

"That would be Stephanson's style," Crandall agreed, as they paid their check and walked past the faces which were just now beginning to turn white. "He'd never do it himself. He'd hire a bully-boy. And he'd do the hiring through an intermediary just in case the bully-boy ever got caught and blabbed. But that still wouldn't be safe enough: he wouldn't want to risk a post-criminal murder charge.

"A dose of Venusian dandelion, he'd figure, and he wouldn't have to worry about me for the rest of my life. He might even come to visit me in the home for incurables—like the way he sent me a card every Christmas of my sentence. Always the same message: 'Still mad? Love, Freddy.'"

"Quite a guy, this Stephanson," Blotto Otto said, peering around the entrance carefully before stepping out of the bar and onto the fifteenth level walkway.

"Yeah, quite a guy. He's got the world by the tail and every once in a while, just for fun, he twists the tail. I learned how he operated when we were roommates way back in college, but do you think that did me any good? I ran into him just when that wholesale electronics business with Irv was really falling apart, about two years after I broke up with Polly.

"I was feeling blue and I wanted to talk to someone, so I told him all about how my partner was a penny-watcher and I was a big dreamer, and how between us we were turning a possible nice small business into a definite big bankruptcy. And then I got onto this remote-control switch I'd been fooling around with and how I wished I had time to develop it."

Blotto Otto kept glancing around uneasily, not from dread of another assassin, but out of the unexpected sensation of doing so much walking of his own free will. Several passersby turned around to have another stare at their out-of-fashion knee-length tunics.

"So there I was," Crandall went on. "I was a fool, I know, but take my word, Otto, you have no idea how persuasive and friendly a guy like Freddy Stephanson can be. He tells me he has this house in the country he isn't using right now and there's a complete electronics lab in the basement. It's all mine, if I want it, as long as I want it, starting next week; all I have to worry about is feeding myself. And he doesn't want any rent or anything—it's for old time's sake and because he wants to see me do something really big in the world.

"How smart could I be with a con-artist like that? It wasn't till two years later that I realized he must have had the electronics lab installed the same week I was asking Irv to buy me out of the business for a couple of hundred credits. After all, what would Stephanson, the owner of a brokerage firm, be doing with an electronics lab of his own? But who figures such things when an old roommate's so warm and friendly and interested in you?"

Otto sighed. "So he comes up to see you every few weeks. And then, about a month after you've got it all finished and working, he locks you out of the place and moves all your papers and stuff to another joint. And he tells you he'll have it patented long before you can get it all down on paper again, and anyhow it was his place—he can always claim he was subsidizing you. Then he laughs in your face, just like Elsa. Huh, Nick?"

Crandall bit his lip as he realized how thoroughly Otto Henck must have memorized the material. How many times had they gone over each other's planned revenge and the situations which had motivated it? How many times had they told and retold the same bitter stories to each other, elicited the same responses from each other, the same questions, the same agreements and even the very same disagreements?

Suddenly, he wanted to get away from the little man and enjoy the luxury of loneliness. He saw the sparkling roof of a hotel two levels down.

"Think I'll move into that. Ought to be thinking about a place to sleep tonight."

Otto nodded at his mood rather than at his statement. "Sure. I know just how you feel. But that's pretty plush, Nick: The Capricorn-Ritz. At least twelve credits a day."

"So what? I can live high for a week, if I want to. And with my background, I can always pick up a fast job as soon as I get low. I want something plush for tonight, Blotto Otto."

"Okay, okay. You got my address, huh, Nick? I'll be at my cousin's place."

"I have it, all right. Luck with Elsa, Otto."

"Thanks, Luck with Freddy. Uh—so long." The little man turned abruptly and entered a main street elevator. When the doors slid shut, Crandall found that he was feeling very uncomfortable. Henck had meant more to him than his own brother. Well, after all, he'd been with Henck day and night for a long time now. And he hadn't seen Dan for—how long was it?—almost nine years.

He reflected on how little he was attached to the world, if you excluded the rather negative desire of removing Stephanson from it. One thing he should get soon was a girl—almost any girl.

But, come to think of it, there was something he needed even more.

He walked swiftly to the nearest drugstore. It was a large one, part of a chain. And there, featured prominently in the window, was exactly what he wanted.

At the cigar counter, he said to the clerk: "It's pretty cheap. Do they work all right?"

The clerk drew himself up. "Before we put an item on sale, sir, it is tested thoroughly. We are the largest retail outlet in the Solar System—*that's* why it's so cheap."

"All right. Give me the medium-sized one. And two boxes of cartridges."

With the blaster in his possession, he felt much more secure. He had a good deal of confidence—based on years of escaping creatures with hair-trigger nervous systems—in his ability to duck and wriggle and jump to one side. But it

66

would be nice to be able to fight back. And how did he know how soon Stephanson would try again?

He registered under a false name, a ruse he thought of at the last moment. That it wasn't worth much, as ruses went, he found out when the bellhop, after being tipped, said: "Thank you, Mr. Crandall. I hope you get your victim, sir."

So he was a celebrity. Probably everyone in the world knew exactly what he looked like. All of which might make it a bit more difficult to get at Stephanson.

While he was taking a bath, he asked the television set to check through Information's file on the man. Stephanson had been rich and moderately important seven years ago; with the Stephanson Switch—how do you like that, the *Stephanson* Switch!—he must be even richer now and much more important.

He was. The television set informed Crandall that in the last calendar month, there were sixteen news items relating to Frederick Stoddard Stephanson. Crandall considered, then asked for the most recent.

That was datelined today. "Frederick Stephanson, the president of the Stephanson Investment Trust and Stephanson Electronics Corporation, left early this morning for his hunting lodge in Central Tibet. He expects to remain there for at least—"

"That's enough!" Crandall called through the bathroom door.

Stephanson was scared! The arrogant bean-pole was frightened silly! That was something; in fact, it was a large part of the return on those seven years. Let him seethe in his own sweat for a while, until he found the actual killing, when it did come at last, almost welcome.

Crandall asked the set for the fresh news and was immediately treated to a bulletin about himself and how he had registered at the Capricorn-Ritz under the name of Alexander Smathers. "But neither is the correct name, ladies and gentlemen," the playback rolled out unctuously. "Neither Nicholas Crandall nor Alexander Smathers is the right name for this man. There is only one name for that man—and that name is death! Yes, the grim reaper has taken up residence at the Ritz-Capricorn Hotel tonight, and only he knows which one of us will not see another sunrise. That man, that grim reaper, that deputy of death, is the only one among us who knows—"

"Shut up!" Crandall yelled, exasperated. He had almost forgotten the kind of punishment a free man was forced to endure.

The private phone circuit on the television screen lit up.

He dried himself, hurried into clothes and asked, "Who's calling?"

"Mrs. Nicholas Crandall," said the operator's voice.

He stared at the blank screen for a moment, absolutely thunderstruck. Polly! Where in the world had she come from? And how did she know where he was? No, the last part was easy—he was a celebrity.

"Put her on," he said at last.

Polly's face filled the screen. Crandall studied her quizzically. She'd aged a bit, but possibly it wasn't obvious at anything but this magnification.

As if she realized it herself, Polly adjusted the controls on her set and her face dwindled to life-size, the rest of her body as well as her surroundings coming into the picture. She was evidently in the living room of her home; it looked like a low-to-middle-income-range furnished apartment. But she looked good—awfully good. There were such warm memories . . .

"Hi, Polly. What's this all about? You're the last person I expected to call me."

"Hello, Nick." She lifted her hand to her mouth and stared over its knuckles for some time at him. Then: "Nick. Please. Please don't play games with me."

He dropped into a chair. "Huh?"

She began to cry. "Oh, Nick! *Don't!* Don't be that cruel! I know why you served that sentence—those seven years. The moment I heard your name today, I knew why you did it. But, Nick, it was only one man—just one man, Nick!"

"Just one man *what?*"

"It was just that one man I was unfaithful with. And I thought he loved me, Nick. I wouldn't have divorced you if I'd known what he was really like. But you know, Nick, don't you? You know how much he made me suffer. I've been punished enough. Don't kill me, Nick! Please don't kill me!"

"Listen, Polly," he began, completely confused. "Polly girl, for heaven's sake—"

"Nick!" she gulped hysterically. "Nick, it was over eleven years ago—ten, at least. Don't kill me for that, please, Nick! Nick, truly, I wasn't unfaithful to you for more than a year, two years at the most. Truly, Nick! And, Nick, it was only that one affair—the others didn't count. They were just—just casual things. They didn't matter at all, Nick! But don't kill me! Don't kill me!" She held both hands to her face and began rocking back and forth, moaning uncontrollably.

Crandall stared at her for a moment and moistened his lips. Then he said, "Whew!" and turned the set off. He leaned back in his chair. Again he said, "Whew!" and this time it hissed through his teeth.

Polly! Polly had been unfaithful during their marriage. For a year—no, two years! And—what had she said?—the others, the *others* had just been casual things!

The woman he had loved, the woman he suspected he had always loved, the woman he had given up with infinite regret and a deep sense of guilt when she had come to him and said that the business had taken the best part of him away from her, but that since it wasn't fair to ask him to give up something that obviously meant so much to him—

Pretty Polly. Polly girl. He'd never thought of another woman in all their time together. And if anyone, anyone at all, had ever suggested—had so much as *hinted*—he'd have used a monkey wrench on the meddler's face. He'd given her the divorce only because she'd asked for it, but he'd hoped that when the business got on its feet and Irv's bookkeeping end covered a wider stretch of it, they might get back together again. Then, of course, business grew worse, Irv's wife got sick and he put even less time in at the office and—

"I feel," he said to himself numbly, "as if I've just found out for certain that there is no Santa Claus. Not Polly, not all those good years! One affair! And the others were just casual things!"

The telephone circuit went off again. "Who is it?" he snarled.

"Mr. Edward Ballaskia."

"What's he want?" Not *Polly, not Pretty Polly!*

An extremely fat man came on the sceen. He looked to right and left cautiously. "I must ask you, Mr. Crandall, if you are positive that this line isn't tapped."

"What the hell do you want?" Crandall found himself wishing that the fat man were here in person. He'd love to sail into sombody right now.

Mr. Edward Ballaskia shook his head disapprovingly, his jowls jiggling slowly behind the rest of his face. "Well, then, sir, if you won't give me your assurances, I am forced to take a chance. I am calling, Mr. Crandall, to ask you to forgive your enemies, to turn the other cheek. I am asking you to remember faith, hope and charity—and that the greatest of these is charity. In other words, sir, open your heart to him or her you intended to kill, understand the weaknesses which caused them to give offenses—and forgive them."

"Why should I?" Crandall demanded.

"Because it is to your profit to do so, sir. Not merely morally profitable—although let us not overlook the life

69

of the spirit—but financially profitable. *Financially* profitable, Mr. Crandall."

"Would you kindly tell me what you are talking about?"

The fat man leaned forward and smiled confidentially. "If you can forgive the person who caused you to go off and suffer seven long, seven *miserable* years of acute discomfort, Mr. Crandall, I am prepared to make you a most attractive offer. You are entitled to commit one murder. I desire to have one murder committed. I am very wealthy. You, I judge —and please take no umbrage, sir—are very poor.

"I can make you comfortable for the rest of your life, extremely comfortable, Mr. Crandall, if only you will put aside your thoughts, your unworthy thoughts, of anger and personal vengeance. I have a business competitor, you see, who has been—"

Crandall turned him off. "Go serve your own seven years," he venomously told the blank screen. Then, suddenly, it was funny. He lay back in the chair and laughed his head off.

That butter-faced old slob! Quoting religious texts at him!

But the call had served a purpose. Somehow it put the scene with Polly in the perspective of ridicule. To think of the woman sitting in her frowsy little apartment, trembling over her dingy affairs of more than ten years ago! To think she was afraid he had bled and battled for seven years because of that!

He thought about it for a moment, then shrugged. "Well, anyway, I bet it did her good."

And now he was hungry.

He thought of having a meal sent up, just to avoid a possible rendezvous with another of Stephanson's ball-throwers, but decided against it. If Stephanson was really hunting him seriously, it would not be much of a job to have something put into the food he was sent. He'd be much safer eating in a restaurant chosen at random.

Besides, a few bright lights, a little gaiety, would be really welcome. This was his first night of freedom—and he had to wash that Polly taste out of his mouth.

He checked the corridor carefully before going out. There was nothing, but the action reminded him of a tiny planet near Vega where you made exactly the same precautionary gesture every time you emerged from one of the tunnels formed by the long, parallel lines of moist, carboniferous ferns.

Because if you didn't—well, there was an enormous leech-like mollusc that might be waiting there, a creature which could flip chunks of shell with prodigious force. The shell merely stunned its prey, but stunned it long enough for the leech to get in close.

And that leech could empty a man in ten minutes flat.

Once he'd been hit by a fragment of shell, and while he'd been lying there, Henck— Good old Blotto Otto! Crandall smiled. Was it possible that the two of them would look back on those hideous adventures, one day, with actual nostalgia, the kind of beery, pleasant memories that soldiers develop after even the ugliest of wars? Well, and if they did, they hadn't gone through them for the sake of fat cats like Mr. Edward Ballaskia and his sanctified dreams of evil.

Nor, when you came right down to it, for dismal little frightened trollops like Polly.

Frederick Stoddard Stephanson. Frederick Stoddard—

Somebody put an arm on his shoulder and he came to, realizing that he was halfway through the lobby.

"Nick," said a rather familiar voice.

Crandall squinted at the face at the end of the arm. That slight, pointed beard—he didn't know anyone with a beard like that, but the eyes looked so terribly familiar . . . .

"Nick," said the man with the beard. "I couldn't do it."

Those eyes—of course, it was his younger brother!

"Dan!" he shouted.

"It's me all right. Here." Something clattered to the floor. Crandall looked down and saw a blaster lying on the rug, a larger and much more expensive blaster than the one he was carrying. *Why was Dan toting a blaster? Who was after Dan?*

With the thought, there came half-understanding. And there was fear—fear of the words that might come pouring out of the mouth of a brother whom he had not seen for all these years . . .

"I could have killed you from the moment you walked into the lobby," Dan was saying. "You weren't out of the sights for a second. But I want you to know, Nick, that the postcriminal sentence wasn't the reason I froze on the firing button."

"No?" Crandall asked in a breath that was exhaled slowly through a retroactive lifetime.

"I just couldn't stand adding any more guilt about you. Ever since that business with Polly—"

"With Polly. Yes, of course, with Polly." Something seemed to hang like a weight from the point of his jaw; it pulled his head down and his mouth open. "With Polly. That business with Polly."

Dan punched his fist into an open palm twice. "I knew you'd come looking for me sooner or later. I almost went crazy waiting—and I did go nearly crazy with guilt. But I never figured you'd do it this way, Nick. Seven years to wait for you to come back!"

"That's why you never wrote to me, Dan?"

"What did I have to say? What *is* there to say? I thought I loved her, but I found out what I meant to her as soon as she was divorced. I guess I always wanted what was yours because you were my older brother, Nick. That's the only excuse I can offer and I know exactly what it's worth. Because I know what you and Polly had together, what I broke up as a kind of big practical joke. But one thing, Nick: I won't kill you and I won't defend myself. I'm too tired. I'm too guilty. You know where to find me. Anytime, Nick."

He turned and strode rapidly through the lobby, the metal spangles that were this year's high masculine fashion glittering on his calves. He didn't look back, even when he was walking past the other side of the clear plastic that enclosed the lobby.

Crandall watched him go, then said "Hm" to himself in a lonely kind of way. He reached down, retrieved the other blaster and went out to find a restaurant.

As he sat, poking around in the spiced Venusian food that wasn't one-tenth as good as he had remembered it, he kept thinking about Polly and Dan. The incidents—he could remember incidents galore, now that he had a couple of pegs on which to hang them. To think he'd never suspected—but who could suspect Polly, who could suspect Dan?

He pulled the prison discharge out of his pocket and studied it. *Having duly served a maximum penal sentence of seven years, discounted from fourteen years, Nicholas Crandall is herewith discharged in a pre-criminal status—*

—to murder his ex-wife, Polly Crandall?

—to murder his younger brother, Daniel Crandall?

Ridiculous!

But they hadn't found it so ridiculous. Both of them, so blissfully secure in their guilt, so egotistically certain that they and they alone were the objects of a hatred intense enough to endure the worst that the Galaxy had to offer in order to attain vengeance—why, they had both been so positive that their normal and already demonstrated cunning had deserted them and they had completely misread the warmth in his eyes! Either one could have switched confessions in mid-explanation. If they had only not been so preoccupied with self and had noted his astonishment in time, either or both of them could still be deceiving him!

Out of the corner of his eye, he saw that a woman was standing near his table. She had been reading his discharge over his shoulder. He leaned back and took her in while she stood and smiled at him.

She was fantastically beautiful. That is, she had everything a woman needs for great beauty—figure, facial structure, complexion, carriage, eyes, hair, all these to perfection—but she had those other final touches that, as in all kinds of art, make the difference between a merely great work and an all-time masterpiece. Those final touches included such things as sufficient wealth to create the ultimate setting in coiffure and gown, as well as the single Saturnian *paeaea* stone glowing in priceless black splendor between her breasts. Those final touches included the substantial feminine intelligence that beat in her steady eyes; and the somewhat overbred, overindulged, overspoiled quality mixed in with it was the very last piquant fillip of a positively brilliant composition in the human medium.

"May I sit with you, Mr. Crandall?" she asked in a voice of which no more could be said than that it fitted the rest of her.

Rather amused, but more exhilarated than amused, he slid over on the restaurant couch. She sat down like an empress taking her throne before the eyes of a hundred tributary kings.

Crandall knew, within approximate limits, who she was and what she wanted. She was either a reigning post-debutante from the highest social circles in the System, or a theatrical star newly arrived and still in a state of nova.

And he, as a just-discharged convict, with the power of life and death in his hands, represented a taste she had not yet been able to indulge but was determined to enjoy.

Well, in a sense it wasn't flattering, but a woman like this could only fall to the lot of an ordinary man in very exceptional circumstances; he might as well take advantage of his status. He would satisfy her whim, while she, on his first night of freedom—

"That's your discharge, isn't it?" she asked and looked at it again. There was a moistness about her upper lip as she studied it—what a strange, sense-weary patina for one so splendidly young!

"Tell me, Mr. Crandall," she asked at last, turning to him with the wet pinpoints on her lip more brilliant than ever. "You've served a pre-criminal sentence for murder. It is true, is it not, that the punishment for murder and the most brutal, degraded rape imaginable are exactly the same?"

After a long silence, Crandall called for his check and walked out of the restaurant.

He had subsided enough when he reached the hotel to

73

stroll with care around the transparent lobby housing. No one who looked like a Stephanson trigger man was in sight, although Stephanson was a cautious gambler. One attempt having failed, he'd be unlikely to try another for some time.

But that girl! And Edward Ballaskia!

There was a message in his box. Someone had called, leaving only a number to be called back.

Now what? he wondered as he went back up to his room. Stephanson making overtures? Or some unhappy mother wanting him to murder her incurable child?

He gave the number to the set and sat down to watch the screen with a good deal of curiosity.

It flickered—a face took shape on it. Crandall barely restrained a cry of delight. He did have a friend in this city from pre-convict days. Good old dependable, plodding, realistic Irv. His old partner.

And then, just as he was about to shout an enthusiastic greeting, he locked it inside his mouth. Too many things had happened today. And there was something about the expression on Irv's face . . .

"Listen, Nick," Irv said heavily at last. "I just want to ask you one question."

"What's that, Irv?" Crandall kept himself rock-steady.

"How long have you known? When did you find out?"

Crandall ran through several possible answers in his mind, finally selecting one. "A long time now, Irv. I just wasn't in a position to do anything about it."

Irv nodded. "That's what I thought. Well, listen, I'm not going to plead with you. I know that after seven years of what you've gone through, pleading isn't going to do me any good. But, believe me or not, I didn't start dipping into the till very much until my wife got sick. My personal funds were exhausted. I couldn't borrow any more, and you were too busy with your own domestic troubles to be bothered. Then, when business started to get better, I wanted to prevent a sudden large discrepancy on the books.

"So I continued milking the business, not for hospital expenses any more and not to deceive you, Nick—really!—but just so you wouldn't find out how much I'd taken from it before. When you came to me and said you were completely discouraged and wanted out—well, there I'll admit I was a louse. I should have told you. But after all, we hadn't been doing too well as partners and I saw a chance to get the whole business in my name and on its feet, so I—I—"

"So you bought me out for three hundred and twenty credits," Crandall finished for him. "How much is the firm worth now, Irv?"

The other man averted his eyes. "Close to a million. But listen, Nick, business has been terrific this past year in the wholesale line. I didn't cheat you out of all that! Listen, Nick—"

Crandall blew a snort of grim amusement through his nostrils. "What is it, Irv?"

Irv drew out a clean tissue and wiped his forehead. "Nick," he said, leaning forward and trying hard to smile winningly. "Listen to me, Nick! You forget about it, you stop hunting me down, and I've got a proposition for you. I need a man with your technical know-how in top management. I'll give you a twenty per cent interest in the business, Nick—no, make it twenty-five per cent. Look, I'll go as high as thirty per cent—thirty-*five* per cent—"

"Do you think that would make up for those seven years?"

Irv waved trembling, conciliatory hands. "No, of course not, Nick. Nothing would. But listen, Nick. I'll make it forty-five per—"

Crandall shut him off. He sat for a while, then got up and walked around the room. He stopped and examined his blasters, the one he'd purchased earlier and the one he'd gotten from Dan. He took out his prison discharge and read it through carefully. Then he shoved it back into the tunic pocket.

He notified the switchboard that he wanted a long-distance Earthside call put through.

"Yes, sir. But there's a gentleman to see you, sir. A Mr. Otto Henck."

"Send him up. And put the call in on my screen as soon as it goes through, please, Miss."

A few moments later, Blotto Otto entered his room. He was drunk, but carried it, as he always did, remarkably well.

"What do you think, Nick? What the hell do you—"

"Sh-h-h," Crandall warned him. "My call's coming in."

The Tibetan operator said, "Go ahead, New York," and Frederick Stoddard Stephanson appeared on the screen. The man had aged more than any of the others Crandall had seen tonight. Although you never could tell with Stephanson: he always looked older when he was working out a complex deal.

Stephanson didn't say anything; he merely pursed his lips at Crandall and waited. Behind him and around him was a TV Spectacular's idea of a hunting lodge.

"All right, Freddy," Crandall said. "What I have to say won't take long. You might as well call off your dogs and stop taking chances trying to kill and/or injure me. As of this moment, I don't even have a grudge against you."

"You don't even have a grudge—" Stephanson regained his rigid self-control. "Why not?"

"Because—oh, because a lot of things. Because killing you just wouldn't be seven hellish years of satisfaction, now that I'm face to face with it. And because you didn't do any more to me than practically everybody else has done—from the cradle, for all I know. Because I've decided I'm a natural born sucker: that's just the way I'm constructed. All you did was take your kind of advantage of my kind of construction."

Stephanson leaned forward, peered intently, then relaxed and crossed his arms. "You're actually telling the truth!"

"Of course I'm telling the truth! You see these?" He held up the two blasters. "I'm getting rid of these tonight. From now on, I'll be unarmed. I don't want to have the least thing to do with weighing human life in the balance."

The other man ran an index nail under a thumb nail thoughtfully a couple of times. "I'll tell you what," he said. "If you mean what you say—and I think you do— maybe we can work out something. An arrangement, say, to pay you a bit —We'll see."

"When you don't have to?" Crandall was astonished. "But why didn't you make me an offer before this?"

"Because I don't like to be forced to do anything. Up to now, I was fighting force with more force."

Crandall considered the point. "I don't get it. But maybe that's the way you're constructed. Well, we'll see, as you said."

When he rose to face Henck, the little man was still shaking his head slowly, dazedly, intent only on his own problem. "What do you think, Nick? Elsa went on a sightseeing jaunt to the Moon last month. The line to her oxygen helmet got clogged, see, and she died of suffocation before they could do anything about it. Isn't that a *hell* of thing, Nick? One month before I finish my sentence—she couldn't wait one lousy little month! I bet she died laughing at me!"

Crandall put his arm around him. "Let's go out for a walk, Blotto Otto. We both need the exercise."

Funny how the capacity for murder affected people, he thought. There was Polly's way—and Dan's. There was old Irv bargaining frantically but still shrewdly for his life. Mr. Edward Ballaskia—and that girl in the restaurant. And there was Freddy Stephanson, the only intended victim—and the only one who wouldn't beg.

He wouldn't beg, but he might be willing to hand out largesse. Could Crandall accept what amounted to charity from

Stephanson? He shrugged. Who knew what he or anyone else could or could not do?

"What do we do now, Nick?" Blotto Otto was demanding petulantly once they got outside the hotel. "That's what I want to know—what do we do?"

"Well, I'm going to do this," Crandall told him, taking a blaster in each hand. "Just this." He threw the gleaming weapons, right hand, left hand, at the transparent window walls that ran around the luxurious lobby of the Ritz-Capricorn. They struck *thunk* and then *thunk* again. The windows crashed down in long, pointed daggers. The people in the lobby swung around with their mouths open.

A policeman ran up, his badge jingling against his metallic uniform. He seized Crandall.

"I saw you! I saw you do that! You'll get thirty days for it!"

"Hm," said Crandall. "Thirty days?" He pulled his prison discharge out of his pocket and handed it to the policeman. "I tell you what we'll do, officer—Just punch the proper number of holes in this document or tear off what seems to you a proportionately sized coupon. Either or both. Handle it any way you like."

The Sickness

For the record, it was a Russian, Nicolai Belov, who found it and brought it back to the ship. He found it in the course of a routine geological survey he was making some six miles from the ship the day after they landed. For what it might be worth, he was driving a caterpillar jeep at the time, a caterpillar jeep that had been made in Detroit, U.S.A.

He radioed the ship almost immediately. Preston O'Brien, the navigator, was in the control room at the time, as usual, checking his electronic computers against a dummy return course he had set up. He took the call. Belov, of course, spoke in English; O'Brien in Russian.

"O'Brien," Belov said excitedly, once identification had been established. "Guess what I've found? Martians! A whole city!"

O'Brien snapped the computer relays shut, leaned back in

the bucket seat and ran his fingers through his crew-cut red hair. They'd had no right to, of course—but somehow they'd all taken it for granted that they were alone on the chilly, dusty, waterless planet. Finding it wasn't so gave him a sudden acute attack of claustrophobia. It was like looking up from his thesis work in an airy, silent college library to find it had filled with talkative freshmen just released from a class in English composition. Or that disagreeable moment at the beginning of the expedition, back in Benares, when he'd come out of a nightmare in which he'd been drifting helplessly by himself in a starless black vacuum to find Kolevitch's powerful right arm hanging down from the bunk above him and the air filled with sounds of thick Slavic snores. It wasn't just that he was jumpy, he'd assured himself; after all, everyone was jumpy . . . these days.

He'd never liked being crowded. Or being taken by surprise. He rubbed his hands together irritably over the equations he'd scribbled a moment before. Of course, come to think of it, if anyone was being crowded, it was the Martians. There was *that*.

O'Brien cleared his throat and asked:

"*Live* Martians?"

"No, of course not. How could you have live Martians in the cupful of atmosphere this planet has left? The only things alive in the place are the usual lichens and maybe a desert flatworm or two, the same as those we found near the ship. The last of the Martians must have died at least a million years ago. But the city's intact, O'Brien, intact and almost untouched!"

For all his ignorance of geology, the navigator was incredulous. "Intact? You mean it hasn't been weathered down to sand in a million years?"

"Not a bit," Belov chortled. "You see it's underground. I saw this big sloping hole and couldn't figure it: it didn't go with the terrain. Also there was a steady breeze blowing out of the hole, keeping the sand from piling up inside. So I nosed the jeep in, rode downhill for about 50, 60 yards— and there it was, a spacious, empty Martian city, looking like Moscow a thousand, ten thousand years from now. It's beautiful, O'Brien, beautiful!"

"Don't touch anything," O'Brien warned. Moscow! Like Moscow yet!

"You think I'm crazy? I'm just taking a couple of shots with my Rollei. Whatever machinery is operating that blower system is keeping the lights on; it's almost as bright as daylight down here. But what a place! Boulevards like colored spider webs. Houses like—like— Talk about the Valley of the

78

Kings, talk about Harappa! They're nothing, nothing at all to this find. You didn't know I was an amateur archaeologist, did you, O'Brien? Well, I am. And let me tell you, Schliemann would have given his eyes—his eyes!—for this discovery! It's magnificent!"

O'Brien grinned at his enthusiasm. At moments like this you couldn't help feeling that the Russkys were all right, that it would all work out—somehow. "Congratulations," he said. "Take your pictures and get back fast. I'll tell Captain Ghose."

"But listen, O'Brien, that's not all. These people—these Martians—they were like us! They were human!"

"Human? Did you say *human*? Like *us?*"

Belov's delighted laugh irradiated the earphones. "That's exactly the way I felt. Amazing, isn't it? They were human, like us. If anything, even more so. There's a pair of nude statues in the middle of a square that the entrance opens into. Phidias or Praxiteles or Michelangelo wouldn't have been ashamed of those statues, let me tell you. And they were made back in the Pleistocene or Pliocene, when saber-tooth tigers were still prowling the Earth!"

O'Brien grunted and switched off. He strolled to the control room porthole, one of the two that the ship boasted, and stared out at the red desert that humped and hillocked itself endlessly, repetitiously, until, at the furthest extremes of vision, it disappeared in a sifting, sandy mist.

This was Mars. A dead planet. Dead, that is, except for the most primitive forms of vegetable and animal life, forms which could survive on the minute rations of water and air that their bitterly hostile world allotted them. But once there had been men here, men like himself, and Nicolai Belov. They had had art and science as well as, no doubt, differing philosophies. They had been here once, these men of Mars, and were here no longer. Had they too been set a problem in co-existence—and had they failed to solve it?

Two space-suited figures clumped into sight from under the ship. O'Brien recognized them through their helmet bubbles. The shorter man was Fyodor Guranin, Chief Engineer; the other was Tom Smathers, his First Assistant. They had evidently been going over the rear jets, examining them carefully for any damage incurred on the outward journey. In eight days, the first Terrestrial Expedition to Mars would start home: every bit of equipment had to be functioning at optimum long before that.

Smathers saw O'Brien through the porthole and waved. The navigator waved back. Guranin glanced upwards curiously, hesitated a moment, then waved too. Now O'Brien hesitated. Hell, this was silly! Why not? He waved at Guranin, a long, friendly, rotund wave.

Then he smiled to himself. Ghose should only see them now! The tall captain would be grinning like a lunatic out of his aristocratic, coffee-colored face. Poor guy! He was living on emotional crumbs like these.

And that reminded him. He left the control room and looked in at the galley where Semyon Kolevitch, the Assistant Navigator and Chief Cook, was opening cans in preparation for their lunch. "Any idea where the captain is?" he inquired in Russian.

The man glanced at him coolly, finished the can he was working on, tossed the round flat top into the wall disposer-hole, and then replied with a succinct English "No."

Out in the corridor again, he met Dr. Alvin Schneider on the way to the galley to work out his turn at K.P. "Have you seen Captain Ghose, Doc?"

"He's waiting down in the engine room, waiting to have a conference with Guranin," the chubby little ship's doctor told him. Both men spoke in Russian.

O'Brien nodded and kept going. A few minutes later, he pushed open the engine-room door and came upon Captain Subodh Ghose, late of the Benares Polytechnic Institute, Benares, India, examining a large wall chart of the ship's jet system. Despite his youth—like every other man on the ship, Ghose was under twenty-five—the fantastic responsibilities he was carrying had ground two black holes into the flesh under the captain's eyes. They made him look perpetually strained. Which he was, O'Brien reflected, and no two ways about it.

He gave the captain Belov's message.

"Hm," Ghose said, frowning. "I hope he has enough sense not to—" He broke off sharply as he realized he had spoken in English. "I'm terribly sorry, O'Brien!" he said in Russian, his eyes looking darker than ever. "I've been standing here thinking about Guranin; I must have thought I was talking to him. Excuse me."

"Think nothing of it," O'Brien murmured. "It was my pleasure."

Ghose smiled, then turned it off abruptly. "I better not let it happen again. As I was saying, I hope Belov has enough sense to control his curiosity and not touch anything."

"He said he wouldn't. Don't worry, Captain, Belov is a bright boy. He's like the rest of us; we're all bright boys."

"An operating city like that," the tall Indian brooded. "There might be life there still—he might set off an alarm and start up something unimaginable. For all we know, there might be automatic armament in the place, bombs, anything. Belov could get himself blown up, and us too. There might be enough in that one city to blow up all of Mars."

"Oh, I don't know about that," O'Brien suggested. "I think that's going a little too far. I think you have bombs on the brain, Captain."

Ghose stared at him soberly. "I have, Mr. O'Brien. That's a fact."

O'Brien felt himself blushing. To change the subject, he said: "I'd like to borrow Smathers for a couple of hours. The computers seem to be working fine, but I want to spot-check a couple of circuits, just for the hell of it."

"I'll ask Guranin if he can spare him. You can't use your assistant?"

The navigator grimaced. "Kolevitch isn't half the electronics man that Smathers is. He's a damn good mathematician, but not much more."

Ghose studied him, as if trying to decide whether or not that was the only obstacle. "I suppose so. But that reminds me. I'm going to have to ask you to remain in the ship until we lift for Earth."

"Oh, no, Captain! I'd like to stretch my legs. And I've as much right as anyone to—to walk the surface of another world." His phraseology made O'Brien a bit self-conscious, but dammit, he reflected, he hadn't come forty million miles just to look at the place through portholes.

"You can stretch your legs inside the ship. You know and I know that walking around in a space-suit is no particularly pleasant exercise. And as for being on the surface of another world, you've already done that, O'Brien, yesterday, in the ceremony where we laid down the marker."

O'Brien glanced past him to the engine room porthole. Through it, he could see the small white pyramid they had planted outside. On each of its three sides was the same message in a different language: English, Russian, Hindustani. *First Terrestrial Expedition to Mars. In the Name of Human Life.*

Cute touch, that. And typically Indian. But pathetic. Like everything else about this expedition, plain pathetic.

"You're too valuable to risk, O'Brien," Ghose was explaining. "We found that out on the way here. No human brain can extemporize suddenly necessary course changes with the speed and accuracy of those computers. And, since you helped design them, no one can handle those computers as well as you. So my order stands."

"Oh, come now, it's not that bad: you'd always have Kolevitch."

"As *you* remarked just a moment ago, Semyon Kolevitch isn't enough of an electronic technician. If anything went wrong with the computers, we'd have to call in Smathers and use the two of them in tandem—not the most efficient working arrangement there is. And I suspect that Smathers plus Kolevitch still would not quite equal Preston O'Brien. No, I'm sorry, but I'm afraid we can't take chances: you're too close to being indispensable."

"All right," O'Brien said softly. "The order stands. But allow me a small disagreement, Captain. You know and I know that there's only one indispensable man aboard this ship. And it isn't me."

Ghose grunted and turned away. Guranin and Smathers came in, having shed their space suits in the air-lock at the belly of the craft. The captain and the chief engineer had a brief English colloquy, at the end of which, with only the barest resistance, Guranin agreed to lend Smathers to O'Brien.

"But I'll need him back by three at the latest."

"You'll have him," O'Brien promised in Russian and led Smathers out. Behind him, Guranin began to discuss engine repair problems with the captain.

"I'm surprised he didn't make you fill out a requisition for me," Smathers commented. "What the hell does he think I am anyway, a Siberian slave laborer?"

"He's got his own departmental worries, Tom. And for God's sake, talk Russian. Suppose the captain or one of the Ivans overheard you? You want to start trouble at this late date?"

"I wasn't being fancy, Pres. I just forgot."

It was easy to forget, O'Brien knew. Why in the world hadn't the Indian government been willing to let all seven Americans and seven Russians learn Hindustani so that the expedition could operate under a mutual language, the language of their captain? Although, come to think of it, Ghose's native language was Bengali. . . .

He knew why, though, the Indians had insisted on adding these specific languages to the already difficult curriculum of the expedition's training program. The idea was that if the Russians spoke English to each other and to the Americans, while the Americans spoke and replied in Russian, the whole affair might achieve something useful in the ship's microcosm even if it failed in its macrocosmic political objectives. And then, having returned to Earth and left the ship, each of them would continue to spread in his own country the ideas of amity and cooperation for survival acquired on the journey.

Along that line, anyway. It was pretty—and pathetic. But was it any more pathetic than the state of the world at the moment? Something had to be done, and done fast. At least the Indians were trying. They didn't just sit up nights with the magic figure *six* dancing horrendous patterns before their eyes: *six, six bombs, six of the latest cobalt bombs and absolutely no more life on Earth.*

It was public knowledge that America had at least nine such bombs stockpiled, that Russia had seven, Britain four, China two, that there were at least five more individual bombs in existence in the armories of five proud and sovereign states. What these bombs could do had been demonstrated conclusively in the new proving grounds that America and Russia used on the dark side of the moon.

Six. Only six bombs could do for the entire planet. Everyone knew that, and knew that if there were a war these bombs would be used, sooner or later, by the side that was going down to defeat, by the side that was looking forward grimly to occupation by the enemy, to war crimes trials for their leader.

And everyone knew that there was going to be a war.

Decade after decade it had held off, but decade after decade it had crept irresistibly closer. It was like a persistent, lingering disease that the patient battles with ever-diminishing strength, staring at his thermometer with despair, hearing his own labored breathing with growing horror, until it finally overwhelms him and kills him. Every crisis was surmounted somehow—and was followed by a slight change for the worse. International conferences followed by new alliances followed by more international conferences, and ever war came closer, closer.

It was almost here now. It had almost come three years ago, over Madagascar, of all places, but a miracle had staved it off. It had almost come last year, over territorial rights to the dark side of the moon, but a super-miracle, in the form of last-minute arbitration by the government of India, had again prevented it. But now the world was definitely on the verge. Two months, six months, a year—it would come. Everyone knew it. Everyone waited for extinction, wondering jerkily, when they had time, why they did no more than wait, why it had to be. But they knew it had to be.

In the midst of this, with both the Soviet Union and the United States of America going ahead full-blast with rocket research and space travel techniques—to the end that when the time came for the bombs to be delivered, they would be delivered with the maximum efficiency and despatch—in the midst of this, India made her proposal public. Let the two opposing giants co-operate in a venture which both were projecting, and in which each could use the other's knowledge. One had a slight edge in already-achieved space travel, the other was known to have developed a slightly better atomic-powered rocket. Let them pool their resources for an expedition to Mars, under an Indian captain and under Indian auspices, in the name of humanity as a whole. And let the world find out once and for all which side refused to co-operate.

It was impossible to refuse, given the nature of the proposition and the peculiarly perfect timing. So here they were, O'Brien decided; they had made it to Mars and would probably make it back. But, while they might have proven much, they had prevented nothing. The spastic political situation was still the same; the world would still be at war within the year. The men on this ship knew that as well, or better, than anybody.

As they passed the air-lock, on the way to the control room, they saw Belov squeezing his way out of his space-suit. He hurried over clumsily, hopping out of the lower section as he came. "What a discovery, eh?" he boomed. "The second day and in the middle of the desert. Wait till you see my pictures!"

"I'll look forward to it," O'Brien told him. "Meanwhile you better run down to the engine room and report to the captain. He's afraid that you might have pressed a button that closed a circuit that started up a machine that will blow up all of Mars right out from under us."

The Russian gave them a wide, slightly gap-toothed smile. "Ghose and his planetary explosions." He patted the top of his head lightly and shook it uneasily from side to side.

"What's the matter?" O'Brien asked.

"A little headache. It started a few seconds ago. I must have spent too much time in that space-suit."

"I just spent twice as much time in a space-suit as you did," Smathers said, poking around abstractedly at the gear that Belov had dropped, "and I don't have a headache. Maybe we make better heads in America."

"Tom!" O'Brien yelped. "For God's sake!"

Belov's lips had come together in whitening union. Then he shrugged. "Chess, O'Brien? After lunch?"

"Sure. And, if you're interested, I'm willing to walk right into a fried liver. I still insist that black can hold and win."

"It's your funeral," Belov chuckled and went on to the engine room gently massaging his head.

When they were alone in the control room and Smathers had begun to dismantle the computer bank, O'Brien shut the door and said angrily: "That was a damned dangerous, un-called-for crack you made, Tom! And it was about as funny as a declaration of war!"

"I know. But Belov gets under my skin."

"*Belov?* He's the most decent Russky on board."

The second assistant engineer unscrewed a side panel and squatted down beside it. "To you maybe. But he's always taking a cut at me."

"How?"

"Oh, all sorts of ways. Take this chess business. Whenever I ask him for a game, he says he won't play me unless I accept odds of a queen. And then he laughs—you know, that slimy laugh of his."

"Check that connection at the top," the navigator warned. "Well, look, Tom, Belov is pretty good. He placed seventh in the last Moscow District tournament, playing against a hatful of masters and grandmasters. That's good going in a country where they feel about chess the way we do about baseball and football combined."

"Oh, I know he's good. But I'm not that bad. Not queen odds. A *queen!*"

"Are you sure it isn't something else? You seem to dislike him an awful lot, considering your motivations."

Smathers paused for a moment to examine a tube. "And you," he said without looking up. "You seem to *like* him an awful lot, considering *your* motivations."

On the verge of anger, O'Brien suddenly remembered something and shut up. After all, it could be anyone. It could be Smathers.

Just before they'd left the United States to join the Russians in Benares, they'd had a last, ultra-secret briefing session with Military Intelligence. There had been a review of the delicacy of the situation they were entering and its dangerous potentialities. On the one hand, it was necessary that the United States not be at all backward about the Indian suggestion, that before the eyes of the world it enter upon this joint scientific expedition with at least as much enthusiasm and cooperativeness as the Russians. On the other, it was equally important, possibly even more important, that the future enemy should not use this pooling of knowledge and skills to gain an advantage that might prove conclusive, like taking over the ship, say, on the return trip, and landing it in Baku instead of Benares.

Therefore, they were told, one among them had received training and a commission in the Military Intelligence Corps of the U. S. Army. His identity would remain a secret until such time as he decided that the Russians were about to pull something. Then he would announce himself with a special code sentence and from that time on all Americans on board were to act under his orders and not Ghose's. Failure to do so would be adjudged *prima facie* evidence of treason.

And the code sentence? Preston O'Brien had to grin as he remembered it. It was: "Fort Sumter has been fired upon."

But what happened after one of them stood up and uttered that sentence would not be at all funny. . . .

He was certain that the Russians had such a man, too. As certain as that Ghose suspected both groups of relying on this kind of insurance, to the serious detriment of the captain's already-difficult sleep.

What kind of a code sentence would the Russians use? "Fort Kronstadt has been fired upon?" No, more likely, "Workers of the world unite!" Yes, no doubt about it, it could get very jolly, if someone made a real wrong move.

The American MI officer could be Smathers. Especially after that last crack of his. O'Brien decided he'd be far better off not replying to it. These days, everyone had to be very careful; and the men in this ship were in a special category.

Although he knew what was eating Smathers. The same thing, in a general sense, that made Belov so eager to play chess with the navigator, a player of a caliber that, back on Earth, wouldn't have been considered worthy to enter the same tournament with him.

O'Brien had the highest I.Q. on the ship. Nothing special, not one spectacularly above anyone else's. It was just that in a shipful of brilliant young men chosen from the thick cream of their respective nation's scientific *élite*, someone had to have an I.Q. higher than the rest. And that man happened to be Preston O'Brien.

But O'Brien was an American. And everything relative to the preparation for this trip had been worked out in high-level conferences with a degree of diplomatic finagling and behind-the-scenes maneuvering usually associated with the drawing of boundary lines of the greatest strategical significance. So the lowest I.Q. on the ship also had to be an American.

And that was Tom Smathers, second assistant engineer.

Again, nothing very bad, only a point or two below that of the next highest man. And really quite a thumpingly high I.Q. in itself.

But they had all lived together for a long time before the ship lifted from Benares. They had learned a lot about each other, both from personal contact and official records, for how did anyone know what piece of information about a shipmate would ward off disaster in the kind of incredible, unforeseeable crises they might be plunging into?

So Nicolai Belov, who had a talent for chess as natural and as massive as the one Sarah Bernhardt had for the theater, got a special and ever-renewing pleasure out of beating a man who had barely made the college team. And Tom Smathers nursed a constant feeling of inferiority that was ready to grow into adult, belligerent status on any pretext it could find.

It was ridiculous, O'Brien felt. But then, he couldn't know: he had the long end of the stick. It was easy, for *him*.

Ridiculous? As ridiculous as six cobalt bombs. *One, two, three, four, five, six*—and *boom!*

Maybe, he thought, maybe the answer was that they were a ridiculous species. Well. They would soon be gone, gone with the dinosaurs.

And the Martians.

"I can't wait to get a look at those pictures Belov took," he told Smathers, trying to change the subject to a neutral, non-argumentative level. "Imagine human beings walking around on this blob of desert, building cities, making love, investigating scientific phenomena—a million years ago!"

The second assistant engineer, wrist deep in a tangle of wiring, merely grunted as a sign that he refused to let his imagination get into the bad company that he considered all matters connected with Belov.

O'Brien persisted. "Where did they go—the Martians, I mean? If they were that advanced, that long ago, they must have developed space travel and found some more desirable real estate to live on. Do you think they visited Earth, Tom?"

"Yeah. And they're all buried in Red Square."

You couldn't do anything against that much bad temper, O'Brien decided; he might as well drop it. Smathers was still smarting over Belov's eagerness to play the navigator on even terms.

But all the same, he kept looking forward to the photographs. And when they went down to lunch, in the big room at the center of the ship, that served as combination dormitory, mess hall, recreation room and storage area, the first man he looked for was Belov.

Belov wasn't there.

"He's up in the hospital room with the doctor," Layatinsky, his table-mate, said heavily, gravely. "He doesn't feel well. Schneider's examining him."

"That headache get worse?"

Layatinsky nodded. "A lot worse—and fast. And then he got pains in his joints. Feverish too. Guranin says it sounds like meningitis."

"Ouch!" Living as closely together as they did, something like meningitis would spread through their ranks like ink through a blotter. Although, Guranin was an engineer, not a doctor. What did he know about it, where did he come off making a diagnosis?

And then O'Brien noticed it. The mess-hall was unusually quiet, the men eating with their eyes on their plates as Kolevitch dished out the food—a little sullenly, true, but that was probably because after preparing the meal, he was annoyed at having to serve it, too, since the K.P. for lunch, Dr. Alvin Schneider, had abruptly been called to more pressing business.

But whereas the Americans were merely quiet, the Russians were funereal. Their faces were as set and strained as if they were waiting to be shot. They were all breathing heavily, the kind of slow, snorting breaths that go with great worry over extremely difficult problems.

Of course. If Belov were really sick, if Belov went out of action, that put them at a serious disadvantage relative to the Americans. It cut their strength almost fifteen per cent. In case of a real razzle between the two groups . . .

Therefore, Guranin's amateur diagnosis should be read as a determined attempt at optimism. Yes, optimism! If it was meningitis and thus highly contagious, others were likely to pick it up, and those others could just as well be Americans as Russians. That way, the imbalance could be redressed.

O'Brien shivered. What kind of lunacy—

But then, he realized, if it had been an American, instead of a Russian, who had been taken real sick and was up there in the hospital at the moment, his mind would have been running along the same track as Guranin's. Meningitis would have seemed like something to hope for desperately.

Captain Ghose climbed down into the mess-hall. His eyes seemed darker and smaller than ever.

"Listen, men. As soon as you've finished eating, report up to the control room which, until further notice, will serve as an annex to the hospital."

"What for, Captain?" someone asked. "What do we report for?"

"Precautionary injections."

There was a silence. Ghose started out of the place. Then the chief engineer cleared his throat.

"How is Belov?"

The captain paused for a moment, without turning around.

"We don't know yet. And if you're going to ask me what's the matter with him, we don't know that yet either."

They waited in a long, silent, thoughtful line outside the control room, entering and leaving it one by one. O'Brien's turn came.

He walked in, baring his right arm, as he had been ordered. At the far end, Ghose was staring out of the porthole as if he were waiting for a relief expedition to arrive. The navigation desk was covered with cotton swabs, beakers filled with alcohol and small bottles of cloudy fluid.

"What's this stuff, Doc?" O'Brien asked when the injection had been completed and he was allowed to roll down his sleeve.

"Duoplexin. The new antibiotic that the Australians developed last year. Its therapeutic value hasn't been completely validated, but it's the closest thing to a general cure-all that medicine's come up with. I hate to use anything so questionable, but before we lifted from Benares, I was told to shoot you fellows full of it if any off-beat symptoms showed up."

"Guranin says it sounds like meningitis," the navigator suggested.

"It isn't meningitis."

O'Brien waited a moment, but the doctor was filling a new hypodermic and seemed indisposed to comment further. He addressed Ghose's back. "How about those pictures that Belov took? They been developed yet? I'd like to see them."

The captain turned away from the porthole and walked around the control room with his hands clasped behind his back. "All of Belov's gear," he said in a low voice, "is under quarantine in the hospital along with Belov. Those are the doctor's orders."

"Oh. Too bad." O'Brien felt he should leave, but curiosity kept him talking. There was something these men were worried about that was bigger even than the fear niggling the Russians. "He told me over the radio that the Martians had been distinctly humanoid. Amazing, isn't it? Talk about parallel evolution!"

Schneider set the hypodermic down carefully. "Parallel evolution," he muttered. "Parallel evolution and parallel pathology. Although it doesn't seem to act quite like any terrestrial bug. Parallel susceptibility, though. That you could say definitely."

"You mean you think Belov has picked up a *Martian* disease?" O'Brien let the concept careen through his mind. "But that city was so old. No germ could survive anywhere near that long!"

The little doctor thumped his small paunch decisively. "We have no reason to believe it couldn't. Some germs we know of on Earth might be able to. As spores—in any one of a number of ways."

"But if Belov—"

"That's enough," the captain said. "Doctor, you shouldn't think out loud. Keep your mouth shut about this, O'Brien, until we decide to make a general announcement. Next man!" he called.

Tom Smathers came in. "Hey, Doc," he said, "I don't know if this is important, but I've begun to generate the lousiest headache of my entire life."

The other three men stared at each other. Then Schneider plucked a thermometer out of his breast-pocket and put it into Smathers's mouth, whispering an indistinct curse as he did so. O'Brien took a deep breath and left.

They were all told to assemble in the mess hall-dormitory that night. Schneider, looking tired, mounted a table, wiped his hands on his jumper and said:

"Here it is, men. Nicolai Belov and Tom Smathers are down sick, Belov seriously. The symptoms seem to begin with a mild headache and temperature which rapidly grow worse and, as they do, are accompanied by severe pains in the back and joints. That's the first stage. Smathers is in that right now. Belov—"

Nobody said anything. They sat around in various relaxed positions watching the doctor. Guranin and Layatinsky were looking up from their chess board as if some relatively unimportant comments were being made that, perforce, just had to be treated, for the sake of courtesy, as of more significance than the royal game. But when Guranin shifted his elbow and knocked his king over, neither of them bothered to pick it up.

"Belov," Dr. Alvin Schneider went on after a bit, "Belov is in the second stage. This is characterized by a weirdly fluctuating temperature, delirium, and a substantial loss of coordination—pointing, of course, to an attack on the nervous system. The loss of coordination is so acute as to affect even peristalsis, making intravenous feeding necessary. One of the things we will do tonight is go through a demonstration-lecture of intravenous feeding, so that any of you will be able to take care of the patients. Just in case."

Across the room, O'Brien saw Hopkins, the radio and communications man, make the silent mouth-movement of "Wow!"

"Now as to what they're suffering from. I don't know, and that about sums it up. I'm fairly certain though that it isn't a terrestrial disease, if only because it seems to have one of the shortest incubation periods I've ever encountered as well as a fantastically rapid development. I think it's something that Belov caught in that Martian city and brought back to the ship. I have no idea if it's fatal and to what degree, although it's sound procedure in such a case to expect the worst. The only hope I can hold out at the moment is that the two men who are down with it exhibited symptoms before I had a chance to fill them full of duoplexin. Everyone else on the ship—including me—has now had a precautionary injection. That's all. Are there any questions?"

There were no questions.

"All right," Dr. Schneider said. "I want to warn you, though I hardly think it's necessary under the circumstances, that any man who experiences any kind of a headache—*any* kind of a headache—is to report immediately for hospitalization and quarantine. We're obviously dealing with something highly infectious. Now if you'll all move in a little closer, I'll demonstrate intravenous feeding on Captain Ghose. Captain, if you please."

When the demonstration was over and they had proved their proficiency, to his satisfaction, on each other, he put together all the things that smelled pungently of antiseptic and said: "Well, now that's taken care of. We're covered, in case of emergency. Get a good night's sleep."

Then he started out. And stopped. He turned around and looked carefully from man to man. "O'Brien," he said at last. "You come up with me."

Well, at least, the navigator thought, as he followed, at least it's even now. One Russian and one American. If only it stayed that way!

Schneider glanced in at the hospital and nodded to himself. "Smathers," he commented. "He's reached the second stage. Fastest-acting damn bug ever. Probably finds us excellent hosts."

"Any idea what it's like?" O'Brien asked, finding, to his surprise, that he was having trouble catching up to the little doctor.

"Uh-uh. I spent two hours with the microscope this afternoon. Not a sign. I prepared a lot of slides, blood, spinal fluid, sputum, and I've got a shelf of specimen jars all filled up. They'll come in handy for Earthside doctors if ever we— Oh, well. You see, it could be a filterable virus, it could be a bacillus requiring some special stain to make it visible, anything. But the most I was hoping for was to detect it—we'd never have the time to develop a remedy."

He entered the control room, still well ahead of the taller

man, stood to one side, and, once the other had come in, locked the door. O'Brien found his actions puzzling.

"I can't see why you're feeling so hopeless, doc. We have those white mice down below that were intended for testing purposes if Mars turned out to have half an atmosphere after all. Couldn't you use them as experimental animals and try to work up a vaccine?"

The doctor chuckled without turning his lips up into a smile. "In twenty-four hours. Like in the movies. No, and even if I intended to take a whirl at it, which I did, it's out of the question now."

"What do you mean—*now?*"

Schneider sat down carefully and put his medical equipment on the desk beside him. Then he grinned. "Got an aspirin, Pres?"

Automatically, O'Brien's hand went into the pocket of his jumper. "No, but I think that—" Then he understood. A wet towel unrolled in his abdomen. "When did it start?" he inquired softly.

"It must have started near the end of the lecture, but I was too busy to notice it. I first felt it just as I was leaving the mess hall. A real ear-splitter at the moment. No, keep away!" he shouted, as O'Brien started forward sympathetically. "This probably won't do any good, but at least keep your distance. Maybe it will give you a little extra time."

"Should I get the captain?"

"If I needed him, I'd have asked him along. I'll be turning myself into the hospital in a few minutes. I'd just wanted to transfer my authority to you."

"Your *authority?* Are you the—the—"

Doctor Alvin Schneider nodded. He went on—in English. "I'm the American Military Intelligence officer. Was, I should say. From now on, you are. Look, Pres, I don't have much time. All I can tell you is this. Assuming that we're not all dead within a week, and assuming that it is decided to attempt a return to Earth with the consequent risk of infecting the entire planet (something which, by the way, I personally would not recommend from where I sit), you are to keep your status as secret as I kept mine, and in the event it becomes necessary to tangle with the Russians, you are to reveal yourself with the code sentence you already know."

"Fort Sumter has been fired upon," O'Brien said slowly. He was still assimilating the fact that Schneider had been the MI officer. Of course, he had known all along that it could have been anyone of the seven Americans. But Schneider!

"Right. If you then get control of the ship, you are to try to land her at White Sands, California, where we all got our preliminary training. You will explain to the authorities how I came to transfer authority to you. That's about all, except for two things. If you get sick, you'll have to use your own judgment about who to pass the scepter to—I prefer not to go any further than you at the moment. And—I could very easily be wrong—but it's my personal opinion, for whatever it may be worth, that my opposite number among the Russians is Fyodor Guranin."

"Check." And then full realization came to O'Brien. "But, doc, you said you gave yourself a shot of duoplexin. Doesn't that mean—"

Schneider rose and rubbed his forehead with his fist. "I'm afraid it does. That's why this whole ceremony is more than a little meaningless. But I had the responsibility to discharge. I've discharged it. Now, if you will excuse me, I think I'd better lie down. Good luck."

On his way to report Schneider's illness to the captain, O'Brien came to realize how the Russians had felt earlier that day. There were now five Americans to six Russians. That could be bad. And the responsibility was his.

But with his hand on the door to the captain's room, he shrugged. Fat lot of difference it made! As the plump little man had said: *"Assuming that we're not all dead within a week. . . ."*

The fact was that the political set-up on Earth, with all of its implications for two billion people, no longer had very many implications for them. They couldn't risk spreading the disease on Earth, and unless they got back there, they had very little chance of finding a cure for it. They were chained to an alien planet, waiting to be knocked off, one by one, by a sickness which had claimed its last victims a thousand thousand years ago.

Still— He didn't like being a member of a minority.

By morning, he wasn't. During the night, two more Russians had come down with what they were all now referring to as Belov's Disease. That left five Americans to four Russians—except that by that time, they had ceased to count heads in national terms.

Ghose suggested that they change the room serving as mess hall and dormitory into a hospital and that all the healthy men bunk out in the engine room. He also had Guranin rig up a radiation chamber just in front of the engine room.

"All men serving as attendants in the hospital will wear space-suits," he ordered. "Before they re-enter the engine room, they will subject the space-suit to a radiation bath of maximum intensity. Then and only then will they join the rest of us and remove the suit. It's not much, and I think any germ as virulent as this one seems to be won't be stopped by such precautions, but at least we're still making fighting motions."

"Captain," O'Brien inquired. "What about trying to get in touch with Earth some way or other? At least to tell them what's hitting us, for the guidance of future expeditions. I know we don't have a radio transmitter powerful enough to operate at such a distance, but couldn't we work out a rocket device that would carry a message and might have a chance of being picked up?"

"I've thought of that. It would be very difficult, but granted that we could do it, do you have any way of insuring that we wouldn't send the contagion along with the message? And, given the conditions on Earth at the moment, I don't think we have to worry about the possibility of another expedition if we don't get back. You know as well as I that within eight or nine months at the most—" The captain broke off. "I seem to have a slight headache," he said mildly.

Even the men who had been working hard in the hospital and were now lying down got to their feet at this.

"Are you sure?" Guranin asked him desperately. "Couldn't it just be a—"

"I'm sure. Well, it had to happen, sooner or later. I think you all know your duties in this situation and will work together well enough. And you're each one capable of running the show. So. In case the matter comes up, in case of any issue that involves a command decision, the captain will be that one among you whose last name starts with the lowest letter alphabetically. Try to live in peace—for as much time as you may have left. Good-bye."

He turned and walked out of the engine room and into the hospital, a thin, dark-skinned man on whose head weariness sat like a crown.

By supper-time, that evening, only two men had still not hospitalized themselves: Preston O'Brien and Semyon Kolevitch. They went through the minutiae of intravenous feeding, of cleaning the patients and keeping them comfortable, with dullness and apathy.

It was just a matter of time. And when they were gone, there would be no one to take care of them.

All the same, they performed their work diligently, and carefully irradiated their space-suits before returning to the engine room. When Belov and Smathers entered Stage Three, complete coma, the navigator made a descriptive note of it in Dr. Schneider's medical log, under the column of temperature readings that looked like stock market quotations on a very uncertain day in Wall Street.

They ate supper together in silence. They had never liked each other and being limited to each other's company seemed to deepen that dislike.

After supper, O'Brien watched the Martian moons, Deimos and Phobos, rise and set in the black sky through the engine room porthole. Behind him, Kolevitch read Pushkin until he fell asleep.

The next morning, O'Brien found Kolevitch occupying a bed in the hospital. The assistant navigator was already delirious.

"And then there was one," Preston O'Brien said to himself. "Where do we go from here, boys, where do we go from here?"

As he went about his tasks as orderly, he began talking to himself a lot. What the hell, it was better than nothing. It enabled him to forget that he was the only conscious intellect at large on this red dust-storm of a world. It enabled him to forget that he would shortly be dead. It enabled him, in a rather lunatic way, to stay sane.

Because this was it. This was really it. The ship had been planned for a crew of fifteen men. In an emergency, it could be operated by as few as five. Conceivably, two or three men, running about like crazy and being incredibly ingenious, could take it back to Earth and crash-land it somehow. But one man . . .

Even if his luck held out and he didn't come down with Belov's Disease, he was on Mars for keeps. He was on Mars until his food ran out and his air ran out and the space-ship became a rusting coffin around him. And if he did develop a headache, well, the inevitable end would come so much the faster.

This was it. And there was nothing he could do about it.

He wandered about the ship, suddenly enormous and empty. He had grown up on a ranch in northern Montana, Preston O'Brien had, and he'd never liked being crowded. The back-to-back conditions that space travel made necessary had always irritated him like a pebble in the shoe, but he found this kind of immense, ultimate loneliness almost overpowering. When he took a nap, he found himself dreaming of crowded stands at a World Series baseball game, of the sweating, soggy mob during a subway rush-hour in New York. When he awoke, the loneliness hit him again.

Just to keep himself from going crazy, he set himself little tasks. He wrote a brief history of their expedition for some wholly hypothetical popular magazine; he worked out a dozen or so return courses with the computers in the control room; he went through the Russians' personal belongings to find out

—just for curiosity's sake, since it could no longer be of any conceivable importance—who the Soviet MI man had been.

It had been Belov. That surprised him. He had liked Belov very much. Although, he remembered, he had also liked Schneider very much. So it made some sense, on a high-order planning level, after all.

He found himself, much to his surprise, regretting Kolevitch. Damn it, he should have made some more serious attempt to get close to the man before the end!

They had felt a strong antipathy toward each other from the beginning. On Kolevitch's side it no doubt had something to do with O'Brien's being chief navigator when the Russian had good reason to consider himself by far the better mathematician. And O'Brien had found his assistant singularly without humor, exhibiting a kind of sub-surface truculence that somehow never managed to achieve outright insubordination.

Once, when Ghose had reprimanded him for his obvious attitude toward the man, he had exclaimed: "Well, you're right, and I suppose I should be sorry. But I don't feel that way about any of the other Russians. I get alone fine with the rest of them. It's only Kolevitch that I'd like to swat and that, I'll admit, is all the time."

The captain had sighed. "Don't you see what that dislike adds up to? You find the Russian crew members to be pretty decent fellows, fairly easy to get along with, and that can't be: you know the Russians are beasts—they should be exterminated to the last man. So all the fears, all the angers and frustrations, you feel you should logically entertain about them, are channeled into a single direction. You make one man the psychological scapegoat for a whole nation, and you pour out on Semyon Kolevitch all the hatred which you would wish to direct against the other Russians, but can't, because, being an intelligent, perceptive person, you find them too likable.

"Everybody hates somebody on this ship. And they all feel they have good reasons. Hopkins hates Layatinsky because he claims he's always snooping around the communications room. Guranin hates Doctor Schneider, why, I'll never know."

"I can't buy that. Kolevitch has gone out of his way to annoy me. I know that for a fact. And what about Smathers? He hates all the Russians. Hates 'em to a man."

"Smathers is a special case. I'm afraid he lacked emotional security to begin with, and his peculiar position on this expedition—low man on the I.Q. pole—hasn't done his ego any good. You could help him, if you made a particular friend of him. I know he'd like that."

"A-ah," O'Brien had shrugged uncomfortably. "I'm no psychological social worker. I get along all right with him, but I can take Tom Smathers only in very small doses."

And that was another thing he regretted. He'd never been ostentatious about being absolutely indispensable as navigator and the smartest man on board; he'd even been positive he rarely thought about it. But he realized now, against the background glare of his approaching extinction, that almost daily he had smugly plumped out this fact, like a pillow, in the back of his mind. It had been there: it had been nice to stroke. And he had stroked it frequently.

A sort of sickness. Like the sickness of Hopkins-Layatinsky, Guranin-Schneider, Smathers-everyone else. Like the sickness on Earth at the moment, when two of the largest nations on the planet and as such having no need to covet each other's territory, were about ready, reluctantly and unhappily, to go to war with each other, a war which would destroy them both and all other nations besides, allies as well as neutral states, a war which could so easily be avoided and yet was so thoroughly unavoidable.

Maybe, O'Brien thought then, they hadn't caught any sickness on Mars; maybe they'd just brought a sickness—call it the Human Disease—to a nice, clean, sandy planet and it was killing them, because here it had nothing else on which to feed.

O'Brien shook himself.

He'd better watch out. This way madness lay. "Better start talking to myself again. How are you, boy? Feeling all right? No headaches? No aches, no pains, no feelings of fatigue? Then you must be dead, boy!"

When he went through the hospital that afternoon, he noticed that Belov had reached what could be described as Stage Four. Beside Smathers and Ghose who were still in the coma of Stage Three, the geologist looked wide-awake. His head rolled restlessly from side to side and there was a terrible, absolutely horrifying look in his eyes.

"How are you feeling, Nicolai?" O'Brien asked tentatively.

There was no reply. Instead the head turned slowly and Belov stared directly at him. O'Brien shuddered. That look was enough to freeze your blood, he decided, as he went into the engine room and got out of his space-suit.

Maybe it wouldn't go any further than this. Maybe you didn't die of Belov's Disease. Schneider had said it attacked the nervous system: so maybe the end-product was just insanity.

"Big deal," O'Brien muttered. "Big, big deal."

He had lunch and strolled over to the engine room porthole. The pyramidal marker they had planted on the first day caught his eye: it was the only thing worth looking at in his swirling, hilly landscape. *First Terrestrial Expedition to Mars. In the Name of Human Life.*

If only Ghose hadn't been in such a hurry to get the marker down. The inscription needed rewriting. *Last Terrestrial Expedition to Mars. In the Memory of Human Life—Here and on Earth.* That would be more apt.

He knew what would happen when the expedition didn't return—and no message arrived from it. The Russians would be positive that the Americans had seized the ship and were using the data obtained on the journey to perfect their bomb-delivery technique. The Americans would be likewise positive that the Russians . . .

They would be the incident.

"Ghose would sure appreciate that," O'Brien said to himself wryly.

There was a clatter behind him. He turned.

The cup and plate from which he'd had lunch were floating in the air!

O'Brien shut his eyes, then opened them slowly. Yes, no doubt about it, they were floating! They seemed to be performing a slow, lazy dance about each other. Once in a while, they touched gently, as if kissing, then pulled apart. Suddenly, they sank to the table and came to rest like a pair of balloons with a last delicate bounce or two.

Had he got Belov's Disease without knowing it, he wondered? Could you progress right to the last stage—hallucinations—without having headaches or fever?

He heard a series of strange noises in the hospital and ran out of the engine room without bothering to get into his space-suit.

Several blankets were dancing about, just like the cup and saucer. They swirled through the air, as if caught in a strong wind. As he watched, almost sick with astonishment, a few other objects joined them—a thermometer, a packing case, a pair of pants.

But the crew lay silently in their bunks. Smathers had evidently reached Stage Four too. There was the same restless head motion, the same terrible look whenever his eyes met O'Brien's.

And then, as he turned to Belov's bunk, he saw that it was empty! Had the man gotten up in his delirium and wandered off? Was he feeling better? Where had he gone?

O'Brien began to search the ship methodically, calling the Russian by name. Section by section, compartment by compartment, he came at last to the control room. It too was empty. Then where could Belov be?

As he wandered distractedly around the little place, he happened to glance through the porthole. And there, outside, he saw Belov. Without a space-suit!

It was impossible—no man could survive for a moment unprotected on the raw, almost airless surface of Mars—yet there was Nicolai Belov walking as unconcernedly as if the sand beneath his feet were the Nevsky Prospekt! And then he shimmered a little around the edges, as if he'd been turned partially into glass—and disappeared.

"Belov!" O'Brien found himself yelping. "For God's sake! Belov! *Belov!*"

"He's gone to inspect the Martian city," a voice said behind him. "He'll be back shortly."

The navigator spun around. There was nobody in the room. He *must* be going completely crazy.

"No, you're not," the voice said. And Tom Smathers rose slowly through the solid floor.

"What's happening to you people?" O'Brien gasped. "What *is* all this?"

"Stage Five of Belov's Disease. The last one. So far, only Belov and I are in it, but the others are entering it now."

O'Brien found his way to a chair and sat down. He worked his mouth a couple of times but couldn't make the words come out.

"You're thinking that Belov's Disease is making magicians out of us," Smathers told him. "No. First, it isn't a disease at all."

For the first time, Smathers looked directly at him and O'Brien had to avert his eyes. It wasn't just that horrifying look he'd had lying on the bed in the hospital. It was—it was as if Smathers were no longer Smathers. He'd become something else.

"Well, it's caused by a bacillus, but not a parasitical one. A symbiotical one."

"Symbi—"

"Like the intestinal flora, it performs a useful function. A highly useful function." O'Brien had the impression that Smathers was having a hard time finding the right words, that he was choosing very carefully, as if—as if— As if he were talking to a small child!

"That's correct," Smathers told him. "But I believe I can make you understand. The bacillus of Belov's Disease inhabited the nervous system of the ancient Martians as our stomach bacteria live in human digestive systems. Both are symbiotic, both enable the systems they inhabit to function with far greater effectiveness. The Belov bacillus operates within us as a kind of neural transformer, multiplying the mental output almost a thousand times."

"You mean you're a thousand times as intelligent as before?"

Smathers frowned. "This is very difficult. Yes, roughly a thousand times as intelligent, if you must put it that way. Actually, there's a thousandfold increase in mental powers. Intelligence is merely one of those powers. There are many others, such as telepathy and telekinesis, which previously existed in such minuscule state as to be barely observable. I am in constant communication with Belov, for example, wherever he is. Belov is in almost complete control of his physical environment and its effect on his body. The movable objects which alarmed you so were the results of the first clumsy experiments we made with our new minds. There is still a good deal we have to learn and get used to."

"But—but—" O'Brien searched through his erupting brain and at last found a coherent thought. "But you were so sick!"

"The symbiosis was not established without difficulty," Smathers admitted. "And we are not identical with the Martians physiologically. However, it's all over now. We will return to Earth, spread Belov's Disease—if you want to keep calling it that—and begin our exploration of space and time. Eventually, we'd like to get in touch with the Martians in the —the *place* where they have gone."

"And we'll have bigger wars than we ever dreamed of!"

The thing that had once been Tom Smathers, second assistant engineer, shook its head. "There will be no more wars. Among the mental powers enlarged a thousand times is one that has to do with what you might call moral concepts. Those of us on the ship could and would stop any presently threatening war; but when the population of the world has made neural connection with Belov's bacillus all danger will be past. No, there will be no more wars."

A silence. O'Brien tried to pull himself together. "Well," he said. "We really found something on Mars, didn't we? And if we're going to start back for Earth, I might as well prepare a course based on present planetary poistions."

Again that look in Smathers' eyes, stronger than ever. "That won't be necessary, O'Brien. We won't go back in the same manner as we came. Our way will be—well, *faster*."

"Good enough," O'Brien said shakily and got to his feet. "And while you're working out the details, I'll climb into a space-suit and hustle down to that Martian city. I want to get me a good strong dose of Belov's Disease."

The thing that had been Tom Smathers grunted. O'Brien stopped. Suddenly he understood the meaning of that frightening look he had had first from Belov and now from Smathers.

It was a look of enormous pity.

"That's right," said Smathers with infinite gentleness. "You can't ever get Belov's Disease. You are naturally immune."

Winthrop Was Stubborn

That was the trouble right there. That summed it up.
Winthrop was stubborn.

Mrs. Brucks stared wildly at her three fellow-visitors from the twentieth century. "But he can't!" she exclaimed. "He's not the only one—he's got to think of us! He can't leave us stranded in this crazy world!"

Dave Pollock shrugged his shoulders inside the conservative gray suit that clashed so mightily with the décor of the twenty-fifth century room in which they sat. He was a thin, nervous young man whose hands had a tendency to perspire. Right now, they were extremely wet.

"He says we should be grateful. But whether we are or aren't grateful isn't important to him. He's staying."

"That means we have to stay," Mrs. Brucks pleaded. "Doesn't he understand that?"

Pollock spread his moist palms helplessly. "What difference does it make? He's absolutely set on staying. He *likes* the twenty-fifth century. I argued with him for two hours; I've never seen anyone so stubborn. I can't budge him, and that's all I know."

"Why don't you talk to him, Mrs. Brucks?" Mary Ann Carthington suggested. "He's been nice to you. Maybe you could make him act sensible."

"Hm." Mrs. Brucks patted her hairdo which, after two weeks in the future, was beginning to get straggly. "You think so? Mr. Mead, you think it's a good idea?"

The fourth person in the oval room, a stoutish middle-aged man, whose face bore an expression of a cat that might swallow a canary in the interests of Decency, considered the matter for a moment, and nodded. "Can't do any harm. Might work. And we've got to do *something*."

"All right. So I'll try."

Mrs. Brucks sniffled deep inside her grandmotherly soul. She knew what the others were thinking, weren't quite saying. To them, Winthrop and she were the "old folks"—both over fifty. Therefore, they should have something in common they should be able to communicate sympathetically.

The fact that Winthrop was ten years her senior meant little to Mr. Mead's forty-six years, less to Dave Pollock's thirty-four and in all probability was completely meaningless to Mary Ann Carthington's even twenty. One of the "old folks" should be able to talk sense to the other, they would feel.

What could they see, from the bubbling distance of youth, of the chasms that separated Winthrop from Mrs. Brucks even more finally than the others? It was unimportant to them that he was a tight and unemotional old bachelor, while she was the warm and gossipy mother of six children, the grandmother of two, with her silver wedding anniversary proudly behind her. She and Winthrop had barely exchanged a dozen sentences with each other since they'd arrived in the future: they had disliked each other deeply from the moment they had met in Washington at the time-travel finals.

But—Winthrop was stubborn. That fact remained. Mr. Mead had roared his best executive-type roars at him. Mary Ann Carthington had tried to jog his senility with her lush, lithe figure and most fluttery voice. Even Dave Pollock, an educated man, a high school science teacher with a master's degree in something or other, Dave Pollock had talked his heart out to him and been unable to make him budge.

So it was up to her. Someone had to change Winthrop's mind. Or they'd all be stuck in the future, here in this horrible twenty-fifth century. No matter if she hated it more than anything she'd had to face in a lifetime of troubles—it was up to her.

She rose and shook out the wrinkles in the expensive black dress her proud husband had purchased in Lord & Taylor's the day before the group had left. Try to tell Sam that it was purely luck that she had been chosen, just a matter of fitting the physical specifications in the message from the future! Sam wouldn't listen: he probably boasted all over the shop, to each and every one of the other cutters with whom he worked, about his wife—one of five people selected in the whole United States of America to make a trip five hundred years into the future. Would Sam still be boasting when the six o'clock deadline passed that night and she didn't return?

This time the sniffle worked its way through the cushions of her bosom and exploded tinily at her nose.

Mary Ann Carthington crooned back sympathetically. "Shall I ring for the jumper, Mrs. Brucks?"

"I'm crazy?" Mrs. Brucks shot back at her angrily. "A little walk down the hall, I need that headache-maker? A little walk I can walk."

She started for the door rapidly before the girl could summon the upsetting device which exploded you from one place to another and left you with your head swimming and your stomach splashing. But she paused for a moment and took a last wistful look at the room before leaving it. While it was by no means a cozy five-room apartment in the Bronx, she'd spent almost every minute of her two weeks in the future here, and for all of its peculiar furniture and oddly colored walls, she hated to leave it. At least here nothing rippled along the floor, nothing reached out from the walls; here was as much sanity as you could find in the twenty-fifth century.

Then she swallowed hard, said *"Ah-h!"* with regretful finality and closed the door behind her. She walked rapidly along the corridor, being careful to stay in the exact middle, the greatest distance possible from the bumpy writhing walls on either side.

At a point in the corridor where one purple wall flowed restlessly around a stable yellow square, she stopped. She put her mouth, fixed in a scowl of distaste, to the square. "Mr. Winthrop?" she inquired tentatively.

"Well, well, if it isn't Mrs. Brucks!" the square boomed back at her. "Long time no see. Come right in, Mrs. Brucks."

The patch of yellow showed a tiny hole in the center which dilated rapidly into a doorway. She stepped through gingerly, as if there might be a drop of several stories on the other side.

The room was shaped like a long, narrow isosceles triangle. There was no furniture in it, and no other exits, except for what an occasional yellow square suggested. Streaks of color chased themselves fluently along the walls and ceilings and floors, shifting the predominant hue of the interior up and down the spectrum, from pinkish grey to a thick, dark ultramarine. And odors came with the colors, odors came and filled the room for a brief spell, some of them unpleasant, some of them intriguing, but all of them touched with the unfamiliar and alien. From somewhere behind the walls and above the ceiling, there was music, its tones softly echoing, gently reinforcing the colors and the odors. The music too was strange to twentieth-century ears: strings of dissonances would be followed by a long or short silence in the midst of

103

which an almost inaudible melody might be heard like a harmonic island in an ocean of sonic strangeness.

At the far end of the room, at the sharp apex of the triangle, an aged little man lay on a raised portion of the floor. Periodically, this raised portion would raise a bit of itself still further or lower a section, very much like a cow trying to find a comfortable position on the grass.

The single garment that Winthrop wore similarly kept adjusting itself upon him. At one moment it would be a striped red and white tunic, covering everything from his shoulders to his thighs; then it would slowly elongate into a green gown that trickled over his outstretched toes; and, abruptly, it would contract into a pair of light brown shorts decorated with a complex pattern of brilliant blue seashells.

Mrs. Brucks observed all this with an almost religious disapproval. A man was meant, she felt dimly, to be dressed approximately the same way from one moment to the next, not to swoop wildly from one garment to another like a montage sequence in the movies.

The shorts she didn't mind, though her modest soul considered them a bit too skimpy for receiving lady callers. The green gown, well, she didn't think it went with Winthrop's sex —as *she'd* been brought up—but she could go along with it; after all, if he wanted to wear what was essentially a dress, it was his business. Even the red and white tunic which reminded her strongly and nostalgically of her grand-daughter Debbie's sunsuit was something she was willing to be generous about. But at least stick to *one* of them, show some willpower, some concentration!

Winthrop put the enormous egg he was holding on the floor. "Have a seat, Mrs. Brucks. Take the load off your feet," he suggested jovially.

Shuddering at the hillock of floor which came into being at her host's gesture, Mrs. Brucks finally bent her knees and sat, her tentative rear making little more than a tangent to it. "How—how are you, Mr. Winthrop?"

"Fine, just fine! Couldn't be better, Mrs. Brucks. Say, have you seen my new teeth? Just got them this morning. Look."

He opened his jaws and pulled his lips back with his fingers.

Mrs. Brucks leaned forward, really interested, and inspected the mouthful of white, shining enamel. "A good job," she pronounced at last, nodding. "The dentists here made them for you so fast?"

"Dentists!" He spread his bony arms wide in a vast and merry gesture. "They don't have *dentists* in 2487 A.D. They *grew* these teeth for me, Mrs. Brucks."

"Grew? How grew?"

"How should I know how they did it? They're smart, that's all. A lot smarter than us, every way. I just heard about the regeneration clinic. It's a place where you lose an arm, you go down there, they grow it right back on the stump. Free, like everything else. I went down there, I said 'I want new teeth' to the machine that they've got. The machine tells me to take a seat, it goes one, two, three—and bingo! there I am, throwing my plates away. You want to try it?"

She shifted uncomfortably on her hillock. "Maybe—but I better wait until it's perfected."

Winthrop laughed again. "You're scared," he announced. "You're like the others, scared of the twenty-fifth century. Anything new, anything different, you want to run for a hole like a rabbit. Only me, only Winthrop, I'm the only one that's got guts. I'm the oldest, but that doesn't make any difference —I'm the only one with guts."

Mrs. Brucks smiled tremulously at him. "But Mr. Winthrop, you're also the only one without no one to go back to. I got a family, Mr. Mead has a family, Mr. Pollock's just married, a newly-wed, and Miss Carthington is engaged. We'd all like to go back, Mr. Winthrop."

"Mary Ann is engaged?" A lewd chuckle. "I'd never have guessed it from the way she was squirming round that temporal supervisor fellow. That little blondie is on the make for any guy she can get."

"Still and all, Mr. Winthrop, she's engaged. To a book-keeper in her office she's engaged. A fine, hard-working boy. And she wants to go back to him."

The old man pulled up his back and the floor-couch hunched up between his shoulder blades and scratched him gently. "Let her go back, then. Who gives a damn?"

"But, Mr. Winthrop—" Mrs. Brucks wet her lips and clasped her hands in front of her. *"She* can't go back, *we* can't go back—unless we all go back together. Remember what they told us when we arrived, those temporal supervisors? We *all* have to be sitting in our chairs in the time machine building at six o'clock on the dot, when they're going to make what they call the transfer. If we aren't *all* there *on* time, they can't make the transfer, they said. So, if one of us, if you, for instance, doesn't show up—"

"Don't tell me your troubles," Winthrop cut her off savagely. His face was deeply flushed and his lips came back and exposed the brand-new teeth. There was a sharp acrid smell in the room and blotches of crimson on its walls as the place adjusted to its owner's mood. All around them the music changed to a staccato, vicious rumble. "Everybody wants Win-

105

throp to do a favor for them. What did they ever do for Winthrop?"

"Umh?" Mrs. Brucks inquired. "I don't understand you."

"You're damn tooting you don't understand me. When I was a kid, my old man used to come home drunk every night and beat the hell out of me. I was a small kid, so every other kid on the block took turns beating the hell out of me, too. When I grew up, I got a lousy job and a lousy life. Remember the depression and those pictures of the breadlines? Well, who do you think it was on those breadlines, on every damn breadline in the whole damn country? Me, that's who. And then, when the good times came back, I was too old for a decent job. Night-watchman, berry-picker, dishwasher, that's me. Cheap flophouses, cheap furnished rooms. Everybody gets the gravy, Winthrop got the garbage."

He picked up the large egg-shaped object he had been examining when she entered and studied it moodily. In the red glow of the room, his face seemed to have flushed to a deeper color. A large vein in his scrawny neck buzzed bitterly.

"Yeah. And like you said, everybody has someone to go back to, everybody but me. You're damn tooting I don't have anyone to go back to. *Damn* tooting. I never had a friend, never had a wife, never even had a girl that stayed around longer than it took her to use up the loose change in my pocket. So why should I go back? I'm happy here, I get everything I want and I don't have to pay for it. You people want to go back because you feel different—uncomfortable, out of place. *I* don't. I'm used to being out of place: I'm right at home. I'm having a good time. I'm *staying*."

"Listen, Mr. Winthrop," Mrs. Brucks leaned forward anxiously, then jumped as the seat under her slunk forward. She rose and stood, deciding that on her feet she might enjoy at least minimal control of her immediate environment. "Listen, Mr. Winthrop, everybody has troubles in their life. With my daughter, Annie, I had a time that I wouldn't wish on my worst enemy. And with my Julius— But because I have troubles, you think I should take it out on other people? I should prevent them from going home when they're sick and tired of jumper machines and food machines and—I don't know —*machine* machines and—"

"Speaking of food machines," Winthrop perked up, "have you seen my new food phonograph? The latest model. I heard about it last night, I said I wanted one, and sure enough, first thing this morning a brand new one is delivered to my door. No fuss, no bother, no money. What a world!"

106

"But it's not your world, Mr. Winthrop. You didn't make anything in it, you don't work in it. Even if everything is free, you're not entitled. You got to *belong,* to be entitled."

"There's nothing in their laws about that," he commented absent-mindedly as he opened the huge egg and peered inside at the collection of dials and switches and spigots. "See, Mrs. Brucks, *double* volume controls, *double* intensity controls, *triple* vitamin controls. What a set! With this one, you can raise the oil texture of a meal, say, while reducing its sweetness with that doohickey there—and if you press that switch, you can compress the whole meal so it's no bigger than a mouthful and you're still hungry enough to try a couple of other compositions. Want to try it? I got it set for the latest number by Unni Oehele, that new Aldebaranian composer: *Memories of a Martian Soufflée.*"

She shook her head emphatically. "No, by me, a meal is served in plates. I don't want to try it. Thank you very much."

"You're missing something. Believe me, lady, you're missing something. The first course is a kind of light, fast movement, all herbs from Aldebaran IV mixed with a spicy vinegar from Aldebaran IX. The second course, *Consomme Grand,* is a lot slower and kind of majestic. Oehele bases it all on a broth made from the white *chund,* a native rabbity animal they have on Aldebaran IV. See, he uses only native Aldebaranian foods to *suggest* a Martian dish. Get it? The same thing Kratzmeier did in *A Long, Long Dessert on Deimos and Phobos,* only it's a lot better. More modern-like, if you know what I mean. Now in the *third* course, Oehele really takes off. He—"

"Please, Mr. Winthrop!" Mrs. Brucks begged. "Enough! Too much! I don't want to hear any more." She glared at him, trying to restrain her lips from curling in contempt. She'd had far too much of this sort of thing from her son, Julius, years ago, when he'd been running around with a crazy art crowd from City College and been spouting hours of incomprehensible trash at her that he'd picked up from the daily newspaper's musical reviews and the printed notes in record albums. One thing she'd learned the hard way was how to recognize an esthetic phony.

Winthrop shrugged. "Okay, okay. But you'd think you'd at least want to try it. The others at least tried it. They took a bite of classical Kratzmeier or Gura-Hok, they didn't like it, they spat it out—fine. But you've been living on nothing but that damn twentieth century grub since we arrived. After the first day, you haven't set foot outside your room. And the

107

way you asked the room to decorate itself—Keerist! It's so old-fashioned, it makes me sick. You're living in the twenty-fifth century, lady; wake up!"

"Mr. Winthrop," she said sternly. "Yes or no? You're going to be nice or not?"

"You're in your fifties," he pointed out. "*Fifties,* Mrs. Brucks. In our time, you can expect to live what? Ten or fifteen more years. Tops. Here, you might see another thirty, maybe forty. Me, I figure I'm good for at least another twenty. With the medical machines they got, they can do wonders. And no wars to worry about, no epidemics, no depressions, nothing. Everything free, lots of exciting things to do, Mars, Venus, the stars. Why in hell are you so crazy to go back?"

Mrs. Brucks' already half-dissolved self-control gave way completely. "Because it's my home," she sobbed. "Because it's what I understand. Because I want to be with my husband, my children, my grandchildren. And because I don't *like* it here, Mr. Winthrop, I don't *like* it here!"

"So go back!" Winthrop yelled. The room which for the last few moments had settled into a pale golden-yellow, turned rose-color again in sympathy. "Go the hell back! There's not one of you with the guts of a cockroach. Even that young fellow, what's-his-name, Dave Pollock, I thought he had guts. He went out with me for the first week and he tried everything once. But he got scared too, and went back to his little old comfy room. It's too *dec-a-dent,* he says, too *dec-a-dent.* So take him with you—and go back, all of you!"

"But we *can't* go back without you, Mr. Winthrop. Remember they said the transfer has to be complete on both sides? One stays behind, all stay. We can't go back without you."

Winthrop smiled and stroked the throbbing vein on his neck. "You're damn tooting you can't go back without me. And I'm staying. This is one time that old Winthrop calls the tune."

"Please, Mr. Winthrop, don't be stubborn. Be nice. Don't make us force you."

"You can't force me," he told her with a triumphant leer. "I know my rights. According to the law of twenty-fifth century America, no human being can be forced to do anything. Fact. I tooked it up. You try to gang up on me, carry me out of here, all I do is set up a holler that I'm being forced and *one! two! three!* a flock of government machines show up and turn me loose. That's the way it works. Put that in your old calabash and smoke it!"

"Listen," she said, as she turned to leave. "At six o'clock,

108

we'll all be in the time machine building. Maybe you'll change your mind, Mr. Winthrop."

"I won't," he shot after her. "That's one thing you can be sure of—I won't change my mind."

So Mrs. Brucks went back to her room and told the others that Winthrop was stubborn as ever.

Oliver T. Mead, vice-president in charge of public relations for Sweetbottom Septic Tanks, Inc., of Gary, Indiana, drummed impatiently on the arm of the red leather easy chair that Mrs. Brucks' room had created especially for him. "Ridiculous!" he exclaimed. "Ridiculous and absolutely nonsensical. That a derelict, a vagrant, should be able to keep people from going about their business . . . do you know that there's going to be a nationwide sales conference of Sweetbottom retail outlets in a few days? I've *got* to be there. I absolutely must return tonight to our time as scheduled, no ifs, no ands, no buts. There's going to be one unholy mess, I can tell you, if the responsible individuals in this period don't see to that."

"I bet there will be," Mary Ann Carthington said from behind round, respectful and well-mascaraed eyes. "A big firm like that can really give them what for, Mr. Mead."

Dave Pollock grimaced at her wearily. "A firm five hundred years out of existence? Who're they going to complain to—the history books?"

As the portly man stiffened and swung around angrily, Mrs. Brucks held up her hands and said, "Don't get upset, don't fight. Let's talk, let's think it out, only don't fight. You think it's the truth we can't force him to go back?"

Mr. Mead leaned back and stared out of a non-existent window. "Could be. Then again, it might not. I'm willing to believe anything—anything!—of 2458 A.D. by now, but this smacks of criminal irresponsibility. That they should invite us to visit their time and then not make every possible effort to see that we return safe and sound at the end of two weeks as scheduled—besides, what about their people visiting in *our* time, the five with whom we transferred? If we're stuck here, they'll be stuck in 1958. Forever. Any government worthy of the name owes protection to its citizens traveling abroad. Without it, it's less than worthless: a tax-grabbing, boondoggling, inept bureaucracy that's—that's positively criminal!"

Mary Ann Carthington's pert little face had been nodding in time to his fist beating on the red leather armchair. "That's what I say. Only the government seems to be all machines. How can you argue with machines? The only government *man* we've seen since we arrived was that Mr. Storku who welcomed us officially to the United States of America of 2458.

And he didn't seem very interested in us. At least, he didn't *show* any interest."

"The Chief of Protocol for the State Department, you mean?" Dave Pollock asked. "The one who yawned when you told him how distinguished he looked?"

The girl made a slight, slapping gesture at him, accompanied by a reproachful smile. "Oh, *you.*"

"Well, then, here's what we have to do. One," Mr. Mead rose and proceeded to open the fingers of his right hand one at a time. "We have to go on the basis of the only human being in the government we've met personally, this Mr. Storku. Two, we have to select a qualified representative from among us. Three, this qualified representative has to approach Mr. Storku in his official capacity and lay the facts before him. The facts, complete and unequivocal. How his government managed somehow to communicate with our government the fact that time travel was possible, but only if certain physical laws were taken into consideration, most particularly the law of—the law of —What *is* that law, Pollock?"

"The law of the conservation of energy and mass. Matter, or its equivalent in energy, can neither be created nor destroyed. If you want to transfer five people from the cosmos of 2458 A.D. to the cosmos of 1958 A.D., you have to replace them simultaneously in their own time with five people of exactly the same structure and mass from the time they're going to. Otherwise, you'd have a gap in the mass of one space-time continuum and a corresponding surplus in the other. It's like a chemical equation—"

"That's all I wanted to know, Pollock. I'm not a student in one of your classes. You don't have to impress *me,* Pollock," Mr. Mead pointed out.

The thin young man grunted. "Who was trying to impress you?" he demanded belligerently. "What can you do for me —get me a job in your septic tank empire? I just tried to clear up something you seemed to have a lot of trouble understanding. That's at the bottom of our problem: the law of the conservation of energy and mass. And the way the machine's been set for all five of us and all five of them, nobody can do anything about transferring back unless all of us and all of them are present at both ends of the connection at the very same moment."

Mr. Mead nodded slowly and sarcastically. "All right," he said. "All right! Thank you very much for your lesson, but now, if you don't mind, I'd like to go on, please. Some of us aren't civil service workers: our time is valuable."

"Listen to the tycoon, will you?" Dave Pollock suggested with amusement. "*His* time is valuable. Look, Ollie, my friend,

110

as long as Winthrop goes on being stubborn, we're all stuck here together. And as long as we're stuck here, we're all greenhorns together in 2458 A.D., savages from the savage past. For your information, right now, your time is my time, and vice versa."

"Sh-h-h!" Mrs. Brucks commanded. "Be nice. Go on talking, Mr. Mead. It's very interesting. Isn't it interesting, Miss Carthington?"

The blonde girl nodded. "It sure is. They don't make people executives for nothing. You put things so—so *right*, Mr. Mead."

Oliver T. Mead, somewhat mollified, smiled a slender thanks at her. "Three, then. We lay the facts before this Mr. Storku. We tell him how we came in good faith, after we were selected by a nation-wide contest to find the exact opposite numbers of the five people from his time. How we did it partly out of a natural and understandable curiosity to see what the future looks like, and partly out of patriotism. Yes, patriotism! For is not this America of 2458 A.D. our America? Is it not still our native land, however strange and inexplicable the changes in it? As patriots we could follow no other course, as patriots we—"

"Oh, for God's sake!" the high school teacher exploded. "Oliver T. Mead pledges allegiance to the flag! We know you'd die for your country under a barrage of stock market quotations. You're no subversive, all right? What's your idea, what's your idea?"

There was a long silence in the room while the stout middle-aged man went through a pantomime of fighting for control. The pantomime over, he slapped his hands against the sides of his hand-tailored dark business suit and said: "Pollock, if you don't want to hear what I have to say, you can always take a breather in the hall. *As I was saying,* having explained the background facts to Mr. Storku, we come to the present impasse. We come to point four, the fact that Winthrop refuses to return with us. And we demand, do you hear me?—we *demand* that the American government of this time take the appropriate steps to insure our safe return to our own time even if it involves, well—*martial law* relative to Winthrop. We put this flatly, definitely, unequivocally to Storku."

"Is that your idea?" Dave Pollock asked derisively. "What if Storku says *no?*"

"He can't say no, if it's put right. Authority, I think that's the keynote. It should be put to him with authority. We are citizens—in temporal extension—of America. We demand our rights. On the other hand, if he refuses to recognize our citizenship, we demand to be sent back where we came from. That's the right of any foreigner in America. He can't refuse. We explain the risks his government runs: loss of good will, irreparable damage to future contacts between the two times, his government standing convicted of a breach of good faith, that sort of thing. In these things, it's just a matter of finding the right words and making them good and strong."

Mrs. Brucks nodded agreement. "I believe. You can do it, Mr. Mead."

The stout man seemed to deflate. *"I?"*

"Of course," Mary Ann Carthington said enthusiastically. "You're the only one who can do it, Mr. Mead. You're the only one who can put things so—so *right*. Just like you said, it has to be said good and strong. That's the way *you* can say it."

"I'd, well—I'd rather not. I don't think I'm the best one for the job. Mr. Storku and I don't get along too well. Somebody else, I think, one of you, would be—"

Dave Pollock laughed. "Now, don't be modest, Ollie. You get along with Storku as well as any of us. You're elected. Besides, isn't this public relations work? You're a big man in public relations."

Mr. Mead tried to pour all the hatred in the universe at him in one long look. Then he shot his cuffs and straightened his shoulders. "Very well. If none of you feel up to the job, I'll take it on myself. Be back soon."

"Jumper, Ollie?" Pollock asked as he was leaving the room. "Why not take the jumper? It's faster."

"No, thank you," Mr. Mead said curtly. "I'll walk. I need the exercise."

He hurried through the corridor and toward the staircase. Though he went down them at a springy, executive trot, the stairs seemed to feel he wasn't going fast enough. An escalator motion began, growing more and more rapid, until he stumbled and almost fell.

"Stop, dammit!" he yelled. "I can do this myself!"

The stairs stopped flowing downward immediately. He wiped his face with a large white handkerchief and started down again. After a few moments, the stairs turned into an escalator once more.

Again and again, he had to order them to stop; again and again, they obeyed him, and then sneakily tried to help him along. He was reminded of a large, affectionate St. Bernard he had once had who persisted on bringing dead sparrows and field mice into the house as gifts from an overflowing heart. When the grisly objects were thrown out, the dog would bring them back in five minutes and lay them on the rug with a gesture that said: "No, I really want you to have it. Don't worry about the expense and hard work involved. Look on it as a slight expression of my esteem and gratitude. Take it, go on take it and be happy."

He gave up forbidding the stairs to move finally, and when he reached ground level, he was moving so fast that he shot out of the empty lobby of the building and onto the sidewalk at a tremendous speed. He might have broken a leg or dislocated his back.

Fortunately, the sidewalk began moving under him. As he tottered from right to left, the sidewalk did so too, gently but expertly keeping him balanced. He finally got his footing and took a couple of deep breaths.

Under him, the sidewalk trembled slightly, waiting for him to choose a direction so that it could help.

Mr. Mead looked around desperately. There was no one in sight along the broad avenue in either direction.

"What a world!" he moaned. "What a loony-bin of a world! You'd think there'd be a cop—somebody!"

Suddenly there was somebody. There was the *pop-pop* of a jumper mechanism in operation slightly overhead and a man appeared some twelve feet in the air. Behind him, there was an orange hedge-like affair, covered with eyes.

A portion of the sidewalk shot up into a mound right under the two creatures. It lowered them gently to surface level.

"Listen!" Mr. Mead yelled. "Am I glad I ran into you! I'm trying to get to the State Department and I'm having trouble. I'd appreciate a little help."

"Sorry," the other man said. "Klap-Lillth and I will have to be back on Ganymede in a half-hour. We're late for an appointment as is. Why don't you call a government machine?"

"Who is he?" the orange hedge inquired as they began to move swiftly to the entrance of a building, the sidewalk under them flowing like a happy river. "He doesn't *narga* to me like one of you."

"Time traveler," his companion explained. "From the past. One of the exchange tourists who came in two weeks ago."

"Aha!" said the hedge. "From the *past*. No wonder I couldn't *narga* him. It's just as well. You know, on Ganymede we don't believe in time travel. It's against our religion."

The Earthman chuckled and dug the hedge in the twigs. "You and your religion! You're as much an atheist as I am, Klap-Lillth. When was the last time you attended a *shkoot-seem* ceremony?"

"Not since the last syzygy of Jupiter and the Sun," the hedge admitted. "But that's not the point. I'm still in good standing. What all you humans fail to understand about the Ganymedan religion . . ."

His voice trailed off as they disappeared inside the building. Mead almost spat after them. Then he recollected himself. They didn't have much time to fool around—and, besides, he was in a strange world with customs insanely different from his own. Who knew what the penalties were for spitting?

"Government machine," he said resignedly to the empty air. "I want a government machine."

He felt a little foolish, but that was what they had been told to do in any emergency. And, sure enough, a gleaming affair of wires and coils and multi-colored plates appeared from nothingness beside him.

"Yes?" a toneless voice inquired. "Service needed?"

"I'm on my way to see Mr. Storku at your Department of State," Mr. Mead explained, staring suspiciously at the largest coil nearest him. "And I'm having trouble walking on the sidewalk. I'm liable to fall and kill myself if it doesn't stop moving under me."

"Sorry, sir, but no one has fallen on a sidewalk for at least two hundred years, and that was a highly neurotic sidewalk whose difficulties had unfortunately escaped our attention in the weekly psychological checkup. May I suggest you take a jumper? I'll call one for you."

"I don't *want* to take a jumper. I want to walk. All you have to do is tell this damn sidewalk to relax and be quiet."

"Sorry, sir," the machine replied, "but the sidewalk has its job to do. Besides, Mr. Storku is not at his office. He is taking some spiritual exercise at either Shriek Field or Panic Stadium."

"Oh, no," Mr. Mead moaned. His worst fears had been realized. He didn't want to go to those places again.

"Sorry, sir, but he is. Just a moment, while I check." There were bright blue flashes amongst the coils. "Mr. Storku is doing a shriek today. He feels he has been over-aggressive recently. He invites you to join him."

Mr. Mead considered. He was not the slightest bit interested in going to one of those places where sane people became madmen for a couple of hours; on the other hand, time *was* short, Winthrop *was* still stubborn.

"All right," he said unhappily. "I'll join him."

"Shall I call a jumper, sir?"

The portly man stepped back. "No! I'll—I'll walk."

114

"Sorry, sir, but you would never get there before the shriek has begun."

Sweetbottom's vice-president in charge of public relations put the moist palms of his hands against his face and gently massaged it, to calm himself. He must remember that this was no bellhop you could complain to the management about, no stupid policeman you could write to the newspapers about, no bungling secretary you could fire or nervous wife you could tell off—this was just a machine into whose circuits a given set of vocal reactions had been built. If he had an apoplectic fit in front of it, it would not be the slightest bit concerned: it would merely summon another machine, a medical one. All you could do was give it information or receive information from it.

"I-don't-like-jumpers," he said between his teeth.

"Sorry, sir, but you expressed a desire to see Mr. Storku. If you are willing to wait until the shriek is over, there is no problem, except that you would be well advised to start for the Odor Festival on Venus where he is going next. If you wish to see him immediately, however, you must take a jumper. There are no other possibilities, sir, unless you feel that my memory circuits are inadequate or you'd like to add a new factor to the discussion."

"I'd like to add a— Oh, I give up." Mr. Mead sagged where he stood. "Call a jumper, call a jumper."

"Yes, sir. Here you are, sir." The empty cylinder that suddenly materialized immediately over Mr. Mead's head caused him to start, but while he was opening his mouth to say, "Hey! I changed—" it slid down over him.

There was darkness. He felt as if his stomach were being gently but insistently pulled out through his mouth. His liver, spleen and lungs seemed to follow suit. Then the bones of his body all fell inward to the center of his now-empty abdomen and dwindled in size until they disappeared. He collapsed upon himself.

Suddenly he was whole and solid again, and standing in a large green meadow, with dozens of people around him. His stomach returned to its proper place and squirmed back into position.

"—changed my mind. I'll walk after all," he said, and threw up.

Mr. Storku, a tall, genial, yellow-haired young man, was standing in front of him when the spasms had subsided and the tears ceased to leak from his eyes. "It's such a simple thing, really, Mr. Mead. Just a matter of being intently placid during the jump."

"Easy—easy to say," Mr. Mead gasped, wiping his mouth with his handkerchief. What was the reason Storku always exuded such patronizing contempt toward him? "Why don't you people—why don't you people find another way to travel? In my time, comfort in transportation is the keystone, the very *keystone* of the industry. Any busline, any airline, which doesn't see to it that their passengers enjoy the maximum comfort en route to their destination is out of business before you can bat an eye. Either that, or they have a new board of directors."

"Isn't he *intriguing?*" a girl near him commented to her escort. "He talks just like one of those historical romances."

Mr. Mead glanced at her sourly. He gulped. She was nude. For that matter, so was everyone else around him, including Mr. Storku. Who knew what went on at these Shriek Field affairs, he wondered nervously? After all, he had only seen them before from a distance in the grandstand. And now he was right in the middle of these deliberate lunatics.

"Surely you're being a bit unjust," Mr. Storku suggested. "After all, if an Elizabethan or a man from the Classic Greek period were to go for a ride in one of your horseless carriages or iron horses—to use your vernacular—he would be extremely uncomfortable and exhibit much more physical strain than you have. It's purely a matter of adjustment to the unfamiliar. Some adjust, like your contemporary, Winthrop; some don't, like yourself."

"Speaking of Winthrop—" Mr. Mead began hurriedly, glad both of the opening and the chance to change the subject.

"Everybody here?" An athletic young man inquired as he bounded up. "I'm your leader for this Shriek. On your feet, everybody, come on, let's get those kinks out of our muscles. We're going to have a real fine shriek."

"Take your clothes off," the government man told Mr. Mead. "You can't run a shriek dressed. Especially dressed like that."

Mr. Mead shrank back. "I'm not going to— I just came here to talk to you. I'll watch."

A rich, roaring laugh. "You can't watch from the middle of Shriek Field! And besides, the moment you joined us, you were automatically registered for the shriek. If you withdraw now, you'll throw everything off."

"I will?"

Storku nodded. "Of course. A different quantity of stimuli has to be applied to any different quantity of people, if you want to develop the desired shriek-intensity in each one of them. Take your clothes off, man, and get into the thing. A

116

little exercise of this sort will tone up your psyche magnificently."

Mr. Mead thought it over, then began to undress. He was embarrassed, miserable and more than a little frightened at the prospect, but he had an urgent job of public relations to do on the yellow-haired young man.

In his time, he had gurgled pleasurably over rope-like cigars given him by politicians, gotten drunk in incredible little stinking bars with important newspapermen and suffered the slings and the arrows of outrageous television quiz shows—all in the interests of Sweetbottom Septic Tanks, Inc. The motto of the Public Relations Man was strictly *When in Rome* . . .

And obviously the crowd he had made this trip with from 1958 was composed of barely-employables and bunglers. They'd never get themselves and him back to their own time, back to a world where there was a supply-and-demand distributive system that made sense instead of something that seemed absolutely unholy in the few areas where it was visible and understandable. A world where an important business executive was treated like *somebody* instead of like a willful two-year-old. A world where inanimate objects stayed inanimate, where the walls didn't ripple around you, the furniture didn't adjust constantly under you, where the very clothes on a person's back didn't change from moment to moment as if it were being revolved in a kaleidoscope.

No, it was up to him to get everybody back to that world, and his only channel of effective operation lay through Storku. Therefore, Storku had to be placated and made to feel that Oliver T. Mead was one of the boys.

Besides, it occurred to him as he began slipping out of his clothes, some of these girls looked real cute. They reminded him of the Septic Tank Convention at Des Moines back in July. If only they didn't shave their heads!

"All together, now," the shriek leader sang out. "Let's bunch up. All together in a tight little group, all bunched up and milling around."

Mr. Mead was pushed and jostled into the crowd. It surged forward, back, right, left, being maneuvered into a smaller and smaller group under the instructions and shoving of the shriek leader. Music sprang up around them, more noise than music, actually, since it had no discernible harmonic relationships, and grew louder and louder until it was almost deafening.

Someone striving for balance in the mass of naked bodies hit Mr. Mead in the stomach with an outflung arm. He said

"Oof!" and then "Oof!" again as someone behind him tripped and piled into his back. "Watch *out!*" a girl near him moaned as he trod on her foot. "Sorry," he told her, "I just couldn't—" and then an elbow hit him in the eye and he went tottering away a few steps, until, the group changing its direction again, he was pushed forward.

Round and round he went on the grass, being pushed and pushing, the horrible noise almost tearing his ear-drums apart. From what seemed a greater and greater distance he could hear the shriek leader chanting: "Come on, this way, hurry up! No, that way, around that tree. Back into the bunch, you: everybody together. Stay *together*. Now, backwards, that's right, *backwards*. Faster, *faster*."

They went backwards, a great mass of people pushing on Mead, jamming him into the great mass of people immediately behind him. Then, abruptly, they went forwards again, a dozen little cross-currents of humanity at work against each other in the crowd, so that as well as moving forward, he was also being hurled a few feet to the right and then turned around and being sucked back diagonally to his left. Once or twice, he was shot to the outskirts of the group, but, much to his surprise when he considered it later, all he did was claw his way back into the jam-packed surging middle.

It was as if he belonged nowhere else by this time, but in this mob of hurrying madmen. A shaved female head crashing into his chest as the only hint that the group had changed its direction was what he had come to expect. He threw himself backwards and disregarded the grunts and yelps he helped create. He was part of this—this—whatever it was. He was hysterical, bruised and slippery with sweat, but he no longer thought about anything but staying on his feet in the mob.

He was part of it, and that was all he knew.

Suddenly, somewhere outside the maelstrom of running, jostling naked bodies, there was a yell. It was a long yell, in a powerful male voice, and it went on and on, almost drowning out the noise-music. A woman in front of Mr. Mead picked it up in a head-rattling scream. The man who had been yelling stopped, and, after a while, so did the woman.

Then Mr. Mead heard the yell again, heard the woman join in, and was not even remotely surprised to hear his own voice add to the din. He threw all the frustration of the past two weeks into that yell, all the pounding, shoving and bruises of the past few minutes, all the frustrations and hatreds of his lifetime. Again and again the yell started up, and each time Mr. Mead joined it. All around him others were joining it, too, until at last there was a steady, unanimous shriek from the tight mob that slipped and fell and chased itself all over the enormous meadow. Mr. Mead, in the back of his mind, experienced a child-like satisfaction in getting on to the rhythm they were working out—and in being part of working it out.

It went pulse-beat, pulse-beat, *shriek-k-k-k*, pulse-beat, pulse-beat, *shriek-k-k-k*, pulse-beat, pulse-beat, *shriek-k-k-k*. All together. All around him, all together. It was good!

He was never able to figure out later how long they had been running and yelling, when he noticed that he was no longer in the middle of a tight group. They had thinned out somehow and were spread out over the meadow in a long, wavering, yelling line.

He felt a little confused. Without losing a beat in the shriek-rhythm, he made an effort to get closer to a man and woman on his right.

The yells stopped abruptly. The noise-music stopped abruptly. He stared straight ahead where everybody else was staring. He saw it.

A brown, furry animal about the size of a sheep. It had turned its head and thrown one obviously startled, obviously frightened look at them, then it had bent its legs and begun running madly away across the meadow.

"Let's get it!" the shriek leader's voice sounded from what seemed all about them. "Let's get it! All of us, together! Let's get it!"

Somebody moved forward, and Mr. Mead followed. The shriek started again, a continuous, unceasing shriek, and he joined in. Then he was running across the meadow after the furry brown animal, screaming his head off, dimly and proudly conscious of fellow human beings doing the same on both sides of him.

Let's get it! his mind howled. *Let's get it, let's get it!*

Almost caught up with, the animal doubled on its tracks abruptly, and dodged back through the line of people. Mr. Mead flung himself at it and made a grab. He got a handful of fur and fell painfully to his knees as the animal galloped away.

He was on his feet without abating a single note of the shriek, and after it in a moment. Everyone else had turned around and was running with him.

Let's get it! Let's get it! Let's get it!

Back and forth across the meadow, the animal ran and they pursued. It dodged and twisted and jerked itself free from converging groups.

Mr. Mead ran with them, ran in the very forefront. Shrieking.

119

No matter how the furry brown animal turned, they turned too. They kept getting closer and closer to it.

Finally, they caught it.

The entire mob trapped it in a great, uneven circle and closed in. Mr. Mead was the first one to reach it. He smashed his fist into it and knocked it down with a single blow. A girl leaped onto the prostrate figure, her face contorted, and began tearing at it with her fingernails. Just before everyone piled on, Mr. Mead managed to close his hand on a furry brown leg. He gave the leg a tremendous yank and it came off in his hand. He was remotely astonished at the loose wires and gear mechanisms that trailed out of the torn-off leg.

"We got it!" he mumbled, staring at the leg. *We got it,* his mind danced madly. *We got it, we got it!*

He was suddenly very tired, almost faint. He dragged himself away from the crowd and sat down heavily on the grass. He continued to stare at the loose wires that came out of the leg.

Mr. Storku came up to him, breathing hard. "Well," said Mr. Storku. "Did you have a nice shriek?"

Mr. Mead held up the furry brown leg. "We got it," he said bewilderedly.

The yellow-haired young man laughed. "You need a good shower and a good sedative. Come on." He helped Mr. Mead to his feet and, holding on to his arm, crossed the meadow to a dilated yellow square under the grandstand. All around them the other participants in the shriek chattered gaily to each other as they cleansed themselves and readjusted their metabolism.

After his turn inside one of the many booths which filled the interior of the grandstand, Mr. Mead felt more like himself. Which was not to say he felt better.

Something had come out of him in those last few moments as he tore at the mechanical quarry, something he wished infinitely had stayed at the dank bottom of his soul. He'd rather never have known it existed.

He felt vaguely, dismally, like a man who, flipping the pages of a textbook of sexual aberrations, comes upon a particularly ugly case history which parallels his life history in every respect, and understands—in a single, horrified flash—exactly what all those seemingly innocent quirks and nuances of his personality mean.

He tried to remind himself that he was still Oliver T. Mead, a good husband and father, a respected business executive, a substantial pillar of the community and the local church—but it was no good. Now, and for the rest of his life, he was also . . . this other thing.

He had to get into some clothes. Fast.

Mr. Storku nodded when the driving need was explained. "You probably had a lot saved up. About time you began discharging it. I wouldn't worry: you're as sane as anyone in your period. But your clothes have been cleaned off the field along with all the rubbish of our shriek; the officials are already preparing for the next one."

"What do I do?" Mr. Mead wailed. "I can't go home like this."

"No?" the government man inquired with a good deal of curiosity. "You really can't? Hm, fascinating! Well, just step under that outfitter there. I suppose you'd like twentieth century costume?"

Mr. Mead nodded and placed himself doubtfully under the indicated mechanism as a newly-clad citizen of the twenty-fifth century America walked away from it briskly. "Ye-es. Please make it something sane, something I can wear."

He watched as his host adjusted some dials rapidly. There was a slight hum from the machine overhead: a complete set of formal, black-and-white evening wear sprang into being on the stout man's body. In a moment, it had changed into another outfit: the shoes grew upwards and became hip-length rubber boots, the dinner jacket lengthened itself into a sou'wester. Mr. Mead was perfectly dressed for the bridge of any whaling ship.

"Stop it!" he begged distractedly as the raincoat began showing distinctive sports shirt symptoms. "Keep it down to one thing."

"You could do it yourself," Mr. Storku pointed out, "if your subconscious didn't heave about so much." Nonetheless, he good-naturedly poked at the machine again, and Mr. Mead's clothes subsided into the tweed jacket and golf knickers that had been so popular in the 1920's. They held fast at that.

"Better?"

"I—I guess so." Mr. Mead frowned as he looked down at himself. It certainly was a queer outfit for the vice-president of Sweetbottom Septic Tanks, Inc., to return to his own time in, but at least it was *one* outfit. And as soon as he got home—

"Now, look here, Storku," he said, rubbing his hands together briskly and putting aside the recent obscene memories of himself with as much determination as he could call up. "We're having trouble with this Winthrop fella. He won't go back with us."

They walked outside and paused on the edge of the mead-

121

ow. In the distance, a new shriek was being organized.

"That so?" Mr. Storku asked with no very great interest. He pointed at the ragged mob of nude figures just beginning to jostle each other into a tight bunch. "You know, two or three more sessions out there and your psyche would be in fine shape. Although, from the looks of you, I'd say Panic Stadium would be even better. Why don't you do that? Why don't you go right over to Panic Stadium? One first-rate, screaming, headlong panic and you'd be absolutely—"

"Thank you, but no! I've had enough of this, quite enough, already. My psyche is my own affair."

The yellow-haired young man nodded seriously. "Of course. *The adult individual's psyche is under no other jurisdiction than that of the adult individual concerned.*—The Covenant of 2314, adopted by unanimous consent of the entire population of the United States of America. Later, of course, broadened by the international plebiscite of 2337 to include the entire world. But I was just making a personal, friendly suggestion."

Mr. Mead forced himself to smile. He was distressed to find that when he smiled, the lapels of his jacket stood up and caressed the sides of his chin affectionately. "No offense, no offense. As I've said, it's just that I've had all I want of this nonsense. But what are you going to do about Winthrop?"

"Do? Why nothing, of course. What can we do?"

"You can force him to go back! You represent the government, don't you? The government invited us here, the government is responsible for our safety."

Mr. Storku looked puzzled. "Aren't you safe?"

"You know what I mean, Storku. Our safe return. The government is responsible for it."

"Not if that responsibility is extended to interference with the desires and activities of an adult individual. I just quoted the Covenant of 2314 to you, my friend. The whole philosophy of government derived from that covenant is based on the creation and maintenance of the individual's perfect sovereignty over himself. Force may never be applied to a mature citizen and even official persuasion may be resorted to only in certain rare and carefully specified instances. This is certainly not one of them. By the time a child has gone through our educational system, he or she is a well-balanced member of society who can be trusted to do whatever is socially necessary. From that point on, government ceases to take an active role in the individual's life."

"Yeah, a real neon-lit utopia," Mr. Mead sneered. "No cops to safeguard life and property, to ask direction of even

—Oh, well, it's your world and you're welcome to it. But that's not the point. Don't you see—I'm certain you can see, if you just put your mind to it—that Winthrop isn't a citizen of your world, Storku? He didn't go through your educational system, he didn't have these psychological things, these readjustment courses, every couple of years, he didn't—"

"But he came here as our invited guest," Mr. Storku pointed out. "And, as such, he's entitled to the full protection of our laws."

"And we aren't, I suppose," Mr. Mead shouted. "He can do whatever he wants to us and get away with it. Do you call that law? Do you call that justice? I don't. I call it bureaucracy, that's what I call it. Red-tape and bureaucracy, that's all it is!"

The yellow-haired young man put his hand on Mr. Mead's shoulder. "Listen, my friend," he said gently, "and try to understand. If Winthrop tried to *do* anything to you, it would be stopped. Not by interfering with Winthrop directly, but by removing you from his neighborhood. In order for us to take even such limited action, he'd have to *do*. That would be *commission* of an act interfering with your rights as an individual: what Winthrop is accused of, however, is *omission* of an act. He refuses to go back with you. Well, now. He has a right to refuse to do anything with his own body and mind. The Covenant of 2314 covers that area in so many words. Would you like me to quote the relevant passage to you?"

"No, I would not like you to quote the relevant passage to me. So you're trying to say that nobody can do anything, is that it? Winthrop can keep all of us from getting back to our own time, but you can't do anything about it and we can't do anything about it. One hell of a note."

"An interesting phrase, that," Mr. Storku commented. "If there had only been an etymologist or linguist in your group, I would be interested in discussing it with him. However, your conclusion, at least in regard to this particular situation, is substantially correct. There is only one thing you can do: you can try to *persuade* Winthrop. Up to the last moment of the scheduled transfer, that, of course, always exists as a possible solution."

Mr. Mead brushed down his overly emotional jacket lapels. "And if we don't, we're out of luck? We can't take him by the scruff of the neck and—and—"

"I'm afraid you can't. A government machine or manufactured government official would appear on the scene and liberate him. Without any damage to your persons, you understand."

"Sure. No damage," Mr. Mead brooded. "Just leaving us stuck in this asylum for the rest of our lives, no ifs, no ands, no buts."

Mr. Storku looked hurt. "Oh, come now, my friend: I'm certain it's not that bad! It may be very different from your own culture in many ways, it may be uncomfortably alien in its artifacts and underlying philosophy, but surely, surely, there are compensations. For the loss of the old in terms of family, associates and experiences, there must be a gain in the new and exciting. Your Winthrop has found it so—he's at Panic Stadium or Shriek Field almost every day, I've run into him at seminars and salons at least three times in the past ten days, and I hear from the Bureau of Home Appliances of the Department of Internal Economics that he's a steady, enthusiastic and thoroughly dedicated consumer. What he can bring himself to do—"

"Sure he gets all those gadgets," Mr. Mead sneered. "He doesn't have to pay for them. A lazy relief jack like him couldn't ask for anything better. What a world—*gahhh!*"

"My only point," Mr. Storku continued equably, "is that being, well, 'stuck in this asylum,' as you rather vividly picture it, has its positive aspects. And since there seems to be a distinct possibility of this, it would seem logical for you people to begin investigating these positive aspects somewhat more wholeheartedly than you have instead of retreating to the security of each other's company and such twentieth-century anachronisms as you are able to re-create."

"We have—all we want to. What we want now, all of us, is to go home and to keep on living the lives we were born into. So what it comes down to is that nobody and nothing can help us with Winthrop, eh?"

Mr. Storku called for a jumper and held up a hand to arrest the huge cylinder in the air as soon as it appeared. "Well, now. That's rather a broad statement. I wouldn't quite want to go as far as that without conducting a thorough personal investigation of the matter. It's entirely possible that someone, something, in the universe could help you if the problem were brought to its attention and if it were sufficiently interested. It's rather a large, well-populated universe, you know. All I can say definitely is that the Department of State can't help you."

Mr. Mead pushed his fingernails deep into his palms and ground his teeth together until he felt the top enamel coming off in flakes and grit. "You couldn't possibly," he asked at last, very, very slowly, "be just a little more specific in telling us where to go for help next? We have less than two

124

hours left—and we won't be able to cover very much of the galaxy in that time."

"A good point," Mr. Storku said approvingly. "A very well-taken point. I'm glad to see that you have calmed down and are at last thinking clearly and resourcefully. Now, who —in this immediate neighborhood—might be able to work out the solution of an insoluble problem? Well, first there's the Temporal Embassy which handled the exchange and brought you people here in the first place. They have all kinds of connections, the Temporal Embassy people do; they can, if they feel like it, tap the total ingenuity of the human race for the next five thousand years. The trouble is, they take too much of the long view for my taste. Then there are the Oracle Machines which will give you the answer to any question that *can* be answered. The problem there, of course, is interpreting the answer correctly. Then, on Pluto, there's a convention this week of vector psychologists. If anyone could figure out a way of persuading Winthrop to change his mind, *they* can. Unfortunately, the dominant field of interest in vector psychology at the moment is foetal education: I'm afraid they'd find your Winthrop far too mature a specimen. Then, out around Rigel, there's a race of re-markably prescient fungi whom I can recommend out of my own personal experience. They have a most unbelievable talent for—"

The portly man waggled a frantic hand at him. "That's enough! That's enough to go on for a while! We only have two hours—remember?"

"I certainly do. And since it's very unlikely that you can do anything about it in so short a time, may I suggest that you drop the whole matter and take this jumper with me to Venus? There won't be another Odor Festival there for sixty-six years: it's an experience, my friend, that should just not be missed. Venus always does these things right: the greatest odor-emitters in the universe will be there. And I'll be very happy to explain all the fine points to you. Coming?"

Mr. Mead dodged out of the way of the jumper which Mr. Storku was gesturing down invitingly. "No, *thank* you! Why is it," he complained when he had retreated to a safe dis-tance, "that you people are always taking vacations, you're always going off somewhere to relax and enjoy yourselves? How the hell does any work ever get done in this world?"

"Oh, it gets done," the yellow-haired young man laughed as the cylinder began to slide down over him. "Whenever there's a piece of work that only a human being can do, one of us—the nearest responsible individual with the applicable training—takes care of it. But our personality goals are different from yours. In the words of the proverb: All play and no work makes Jack a dull boy."

And he was gone.

So Mr. Mead went back to Mrs. Brucks' room and told the others that the Department of State, as personified by Mr. Storku, couldn't help them with Winthrop's stubbornness.

Mary Ann Carthington tightened the curl of her blonde hair with a business-like forefinger while she considered the matter. "You told him all that you told us, and he still wouldn't do anything, Mr. Mead? Are you sure he knows who you are?"

Mr. Mead didn't bother to answer her. He had other things on his mind. Not only was his spirit badly bruised and scratched by his recent experiences, but his golf knickers had just woken into sentiency. And whereas the jacket merely had attempted to express its great affection for his person by trying to cuddle under his chin, the knickers went in more for a kind of patrolling action. Up and down on his thighs they rippled; back and forth across his buttocks they marched. Only by concentrating hard and pressing them tight against his body with his hands was he able to keep away the feeling of having been swallowed by an anaconda.

"Sure he knows who he is," Dave Pollock told her. "Ollie waved his vice-presidency in his face, but Storku heard that Sweetbottom Septic Tanks Preferred fell to the bottom of the stock market just 481 years ago today, so he wasn't having any. Hey, Ollie?"

"I don't think that's funny, Dave Pollock," Mary Ann Carthington said and shook her head at him once in a "so, there!" manner. She knew that old beanpole of a schoolteacher was just jealous of Mr. Mead, but she wasn't sure whether it was because he didn't make as much money or because he wasn't nearly as distinguished-looking. The only thing, if a big executive like Mr. Mead couldn't get them out of this jam, then nobody could. And that would be awful, positively and absolutely awful.

She would never get back to Edgar Rapp. And while Edgar might not be everything a girl like Mary Ann wanted, she was quite willing to settle for him at this point. He worked hard and made a good living. His compliments were pale, pedestrian things, true, but at least he could be counted on not to say anything that tore a person into little, worthless bits right before their very eyes. Not like somebody she knew. And the sooner she could leave the twenty-fifth century and be forever away from that somebody, the better.

"Now, Mr. Mead," she cooed insistently. "I'm sure he told you *something* we could do. He didn't just tell you to give up hope completely and absolutely, did he?"

The executive caught the strap end of his knickers as it came unbuckled and started rolling exultantly up his leg. He glared at her out of eyes that had seen just too damn much, that felt things had gone just too damn far.

"He told me something we could do," he said with careful viciousness. "He said the Temporal Embassy could help us, if we only had the right kind of pull there. All we need is somebody with pull in the Temporal Embassy."

Mary Ann Carthington almost bit the end off the lipstick she was applying at that moment. Without looking up, she knew that Mrs. Brucks and Dave Pollock had both turned to stare at her. And she knew, deep down to the bottom of her dismayed intestines, just exactly what they were thinking.

"Well, I certainly don't—"

"Now, don't be modest, Mary Ann," Dave Pollock interrupted. "This is your big chance—and right now it looks like our only chance. We've got about an hour and a half left. Get yourself into a jumper, skedaddle out there, and girlie, turn on the charm!"

Mrs. Brucks sat down beside her and gave her shoulders the benefit of a heavy maternal arm. "Listen, Miss Carthington, sometimes we have to do things, is not so easy. But what else? Stuck here is better? *That* you like? So—" she spread her hands—"a touch here with the powder puff, a touch there with the lipstick, a this, a that, and, believe me, he won't know what to do first for you. Crazy about you he is already—you mean to say a little favor he wouldn't do, if you asked him?" She shrugged her massive contempt for such a sleeveless thought.

"You really think so? Well—maybe—" The girl began a preen that started at her delicately firm bottom and ended in a couple of self-satisfied wriggles somewhere around her chest.

"No maybes," Mrs. Brucks informed her after considering the matter with great care. "A sure, yes. A certainly, yes. But maybes, no. A pretty girl like you, a man like him, nothing to maybe about. It's the way, let me tell you, Miss Carthington, it's always the way. What a man like Mr. Mead can't accomplish, a woman has to do all the time. And a pretty girl like you can do it without lifting her little finger."

Mary Ann Carthington gave a nod of agreement to this

rather female view of history and stood up with determination. Dave Pollock immediately called for a jumper. She stepped back as the great cylinder materialized in the room.

"Do I *have* to?" she asked, biting her lip. "Those awful things, they're so *upsetting*."

He took her arm and began working her under the jumper with a series of gentle, urging tugs. "You can't walk: we don't have the time anymore. Believe me, Mary Ann, this is *D*-day and *it*-hour. So be a good girl and get under there and— Hey, listen. A good angle with the temporal supervisor might be about how his people will be stuck in our period if Winthrop goes on being stubborn. If anyone around here is responsible for them, he is. So, as soon as you get there—"

"I don't need you to tell me how to handle the temporal supervisor, Dave Pollock!" she said haughtily, flouncing under the jumper. "After all, he happens to be a friend of mine, not of yours—a very *good* friend of mine!"

"Sure," Pollock groaned, "but you still have to convince the man. And all I'm suggesting—" He broke off as the cylinder slid the final distance down to the floor and disappeared with the girl inside.

He turned back to the others who had been watching anxiously. "Well, that's it," he announced, flapping his arms with a broad, hopeless gesture. "That's our very last hope. A Mary Ann!"

Mary Ann Carthington felt exactly like a Last Hope as she materialized in the Temporal Embassy.

She fought down the swimming nausea which always seemed to accompany jumper transportation and, shaking her head rapidly, managed to draw a deep breath.

As a means of getting places, the jumper certainly beat Edgar Rapp's gurgling old Buick—if only it didn't make you feel like a chocolate malted. That was the trouble with this time: every halfway nice thing in it had such unpleasant after-effects!

The ceiling undulated over her head in the great rotunda where she was now standing and bulged a huge purplish lump down at her. It still looked, she decided nervously, like a movie house chandelier about to fall.

"Yes?" inquired the purplish lump politely. "Whom did you wish to see?"

She licked at her lipstick, then squared her shoulders. She'd been through all this before. You had to carry these things off with a certain amount of poise: it just did not do to show nervousness before a ceiling.

"I came to see Gygyo—I mean, is Mr. Gygyo Rablin in?"

"Mr. Rablin is not at size at the moment. He will return in fifteen minutes. Would you like to wait in his office? He has another visitor there."

Mary Ann Carthington thought swiftly. She didn't entirely like the idea of another visitor, but maybe it would be for the best. The presence of a third party would be a restraining influence for both of them and would take a little of the inevitable edge off her coming back to Gygyo as a suppliant after what had happened between them.

But what was this about his not being "at size"? These twenty-fifth century people did so many positively weird things with themselves. . . .

"Yes, I'll wait in his office," she told the ceiling. "Oh, you needn't bother," she said to the floor as it began to ripple under her feet. "I know the way."

"No bother at all, Miss," the floor replied cheerfully and continued to carry her across the rotunda to Rablin's private office. "It's a pleasure."

Mary Ann sighed and shook her head. Some of these houses were so opinionated! She relaxed and let herself be carried along, taking out her compact on the way for a last quick check of her hair and face.

But the glance at herself in the mirror evoked the memory again. She flushed and almost called for a jumper to take her back to Mrs. Brucks' room. No, she couldn't—this was their last chance to get out of this world and back to their own. But damn Gygyo Rablin, anyway—damn and damn him!

A yellow square in the wall having dilated sufficiently, the floor carried her into Rablin's private office and subsided to flatness again. She looked around, nodding slightly at the familiar surroundings.

There was Gygyo's desk, if you could call that odd, purring thing a desk. There was that peculiar squirmy couch that—

She caught her breath. A young woman was lying on the couch, one of those horrible bald-headed women that they had here.

"Excuse me," Mary Ann said in one fast breath. "I had no idea—I didn't mean to—"

"That's perfectly all right," the young woman said, still staring up at the ceiling. "You're not intruding. I just dropped in on Gygyo myself. Have a seat."

As if taking a pointed hint, the floor shot up a section of itself under Mary Ann's bottom and, when she was securely cradled in it, lowered itself slowly to sitting height.

"You must be that twentieth century—" the young woman

paused, then amended rapidly: "the *visitor* whom Gygyo has been seeing lately. My name's Flureet. I'm just an old childhood friend—'way back from Responsibility Group Three."

Mary Ann nodded primly. "How nice, I'm sure. My name is Mary Ann Carthington. And really, if in any way I'm—I mean I just dropped in to—"

"I told you it's all right. Gygyo and I don't mean a thing to each other. This Temporal Embassy work has kind of dulled his taste for the everyday female: they've either got to be stavisms or precursors. Some kind of anachronism, anyway. And I'm awaiting transformation—*major* transformation—so you couldn't expect very strong feelings from my side right now. Satisfied? I hope so. Hello to you, Mary Ann."

Flureet flexed her arm at the elbow several times in what Mary Ann recognized disdainfully as the standard greeting gesture. Such women! It made them look like a man showing off his muscle. And not so much as a polite glance in the direction of a guest!

"The ceiling said," she began uncertainly, "that Gyg—Mr. Rablin isn't at size at the moment. Is that like what we call not being at home?"

The bald girl nodded. "In a sense. He's in this room, but he's hardly large enough to talk to. Gygy's size right now is —let me think, what did he say he was setting it for?—Oh, yes, 35 microns. He's inside a drop of water in the field of that microscope to your left."

Mary Ann swung around and considered the spherical black object resting on a table against the wall. Outside of the two eyepieces set flush with the surface, it had little in common with pictures of microscopes she had seen in magazines.

"In—in there? What's he doing in there?"

"He's on a micro-hunt. You should know your Gygyo by now. An absolutely incurable romantic. Who goes on micro-hunts anymore? And in a culture of intestinal amebae, of all things. Killing the beasties by hand instead of by routine psycho or even chemo therapy appeals to his dashing soul. Grow up, Gygyo, I said to him: these games are for children and for Responsibility Group Four children at that. Well, that hurt his pride and he said he was going in with a fifteen-minute lock. A fifteen-minute *lock!* When I heard that, I decided to come here and watch the battle, just in case."

"Why—is a fifteen-minute lock dangerous?" Mary Ann asked. Her face was tightly set however; she was still thinking of that 'you should know your Gygyo' remark. That was another thing about this world she didn't like: with all their

130

talk of privacy and the sacred rights of the individual, men like Gygyo didn't think twice of telling the most intimate matters about people to—to other people.

"Figure it out for yourself. Gygyo's set himself for 35 microns. 35 Microns is about twice the size of most of the intestinal parasites he'll have to fight—amebae like *Endolimax nana, Iodamoeba butschlii* and *Dientamoeba fragilis.* But suppose he runs into a crowd of *Endamoeba coli,* to say nothing of our tropical dysentery friend, *Endamoeba hystolytica?* What then?"

"What then?" the blonde girl echoed. She had not the slightest idea. One did not face problems like this is San Francisco.

"Trouble, that's what. Serious trouble. The *colii* might be as large as he is, and *hystolyticae* run even bigger. 36, 37 microns, sometimes more. Now, the most important factor on a micro-hunt, as you know, is size. Especially if you're fool enough to limit your arsenal to a sword and won't be seen carrying an automatic weapon even as insurance. Well, under those circumstances, you lock yourself down to smallness, so that you can't get out and nobody can take you out for a full fifteen minutes, and you're just asking for trouble. And trouble is just what our boy is having!"

"He is? I mean, is it bad?"

Flureet gestured at the microscope. "Have a look. I've adjusted my retina to the magnification, but you people aren't up to that yet, I believe. You need mechanical devices for everything. Go ahead, have a look. That's *Dietamoeba fragilis* he's fighting now. Small, but fast. And very, very vicious."

Mary Ann hurried to the spherically shaped microscope and stared intently through the eyepieces.

There, in the very center of the field, was Gygyo. A transparent bubble helmet covered his head and he was wearing some sort of thick but flexible one-piece garment over the rest of his body. About a dozen amebac the size of dogs swarmed about him, reaching for his body with blunt, glassy pseudopods. He hacked away at them with a great, two-handed sword in tremendous sweeps that cut in two the most venturesome and persistent of the creatures. But Mary Ann could see from his frantic breathing that he was getting tired. Every once in a while he glanced rapidly over his left shoulder as if keeping watch on something in the distance.

"Where does he get air from?" she asked.

"The suit always contains enough oxygen for the duration of the lock," Flureet's voice explained behind her, somewhat surprised at the question. "He has about five minutes to go, and I think he'll make it. I think he'll be shaken up enough though, to— Did you see *that?*"

Mary Ann gasped. An elongated, spindle-shaped creature ending in a thrashing whip-like streak had just darted across the field, well over Gygyo's head. It was about one and a half times his size. He had gone into a crouch as it passed and the amebae surrounding him had also leaped away. They were back at the attack in a moment, however, once the danger had passed. Very wearily now, he continued to chop at them.

"What *was* it."

"A trypanosome. It went by too fast for me to identify it, but it looked like either *Trypanosoma gambiense* or *rhodisiense*—the African sleeping sickness protozoans. It was a bit too big to be either of them, now that I remember. It could have been— Oh, the fool, the fool!"

Mary Ann turned to her, genuinely frightened. "Why—what did he do?"

"He neglected to get a pure culture, that's what he did. Taking on several different kinds of intestinal amebae is wild enough, but if there are trypanosomes in there with him, then there might be anything! And him down to 35 microns!"

Remembering the frightened glances that Gygyo had thrown over his shoulder, Mary Ann swung back to the microscope. The man was still fighting desperately, but the strokes of the sword came much more slowly. Suddenly, another ameba, different from those attacking Gygyo, swam leisurely into the field. It was almost transparent and about half his size.

"That's a new one," she told Flureet. "Is it dangerous?"

"No, *Iodamoeba butschlii* is just a sluggish, friendly lump. But what in the world is Gygyo afraid of to his left? He keeps turning his head as if— *Oh.*"

The last exclamation came out almost as a simple comment, so completely was it weighted with despair. An oval monster—its length three times and its width fully twice Gygyo's height—shot into the field from the left boundary as if making a stage entrance in reply to her question. The tiny, hair-like appendages with which it was covered seemed to give it fantastic speed.

Gygyo's sword slashed at it, but it swerved aside and out of the field. It was back in a moment, coming down like a dive bomber. Gygyo leaped away, but one of the amebae which had been attacking him was a little too slow. It disappeared, struggling madly, down the funnel-shaped mouth which indented the forward end of the egg-shaped monster.

"Balantidium Coli," Flureet explained before Mary Ann could force her trembling lips to frame the question. "100 microns long, 65 microns wide. Fast and deadly and terribly hungry. I was afraid he'd hit something like this sooner or later. Well, that's the end of our micro-hunting friend. He'll never be able to avoid it long enough to get out. And he can't kill a bug that size."

Mary Ann held quivering hands out to her. "Can't you *do* something?"

The bald woman brought her eyes down from the ceiling at last. Making what seemed an intense effort, she focused them on the girl. They were lit with bright astonishment.

"What can I do? He's locked inside that culture for another four minutes at least; an absolutely unbreakable lock. Do you expect me to—to go in there and *rescue* him?"

"If you can—of course!"

"But that would be interfering with his sovereign rights as an individual! My dear girl! Even if his wish to destroy himself is unconscious, it is still a wish originating in an essential part of his personality and must be respected. The whole thing is covered by the subsidiary—rights covenant of—"

"How do you *know* he wants to destroy himself?" Mary Ann wept. "I never heard of such a thing! He's supposed to be a—a friend of yours! Maybe he just accidentally got himself into more trouble than he expected, and he can't get out. I'm positive that's what happened. Oh—poor Gygyo, while we're standing here talking, he's getting killed!"

Flureet considered. "You may have something there. He is a romantic, and associating with you has given him all sorts of swaggering adventuresome notions. He'd never have done anything as risky as this before. But tell me: do you think it's worth taking a chance of interfering with someone's sovereign individual rights, just to save the life of an old and dear friend?"

"I don't *understand* you," Mary Ann said helplessly. "Of *course*! Why don't you let me—just do whatever you have to and send me in there after him. Please!"

The other woman rose and shook her head. "No, I think I'd be more effective. I must say, this romanticism is catching. And," she laughed to herself, "just a little intriguing. You people in the twentieth century led such lives!"

Before Mary Ann's eyes, she shrank down rapidly. Just as she disappeared, there was a whispering movement, like a flame curving from a candle, and her body seemed to streak toward the microscope.

Gygyo was down on one knee, now, trying to present as

small an area to the oval monster as possible. The amebea with which he had been surrounded had now either all fled or been swallowed. He was swinging the sword back and forth rapidly over his head as the *Balantidium coli* swooped down first on one side, then on the other, but he looked very tired. His lips were clenched together, his eyes squinted with desperation.

And then the huge creature came straight down, feinted with its body, and, as he lunged at it with the sword, swerved slightly and hit him from the rear. Gygyo fell, losing his weapon.

Hairy appendages churning, the monster spun around fluently so that its funnel-shaped mouth was in front, and came back rapidly for the kill.

An enormous hand, a hand the size of Gygyo's whole body, swung into view and knocked it to one side. Gygyo scrambled to his feet, regained the sword, and looked up unbelievingly. He exhaled with relief and then smiled. Flureet had evidently stopped her shrinkage at a size several times larger than a hundred microns. Her body was not visible in the field of the microscope to Mary Ann, but it was obviously far too visible to the *Balantidium Coli* which turned end over end and scudded away.

And for the remaining minutes of the lock, there was not a creature which seemed even vaguely inclined to wander into Gygyo's neighborhood.

To Mary Ann's astonishment, Flureet's first words to Gygyo when they reappeared beside her at their full height were an apology: "I'm truly sorry, but your fire-eating friend here got me all excited about your safety, Gygyo. If you want to bring me up on charges of violating the Covenant and interfering with an individual's carefully prepared plans for self-destruction—"

Gygyo waved her to silence. "Forget it. In the words of the poet: Covenant, Shmovenant. You saved my life, and, as far as I know, I wanted it saved. If I instituted proceedings against you for interfering with my unconscious, in all fairness we'd have to subpoena my conscious mind as a witness in your defense. The case could drag on for months, and I'm far too busy."

The woman nodded. "You're right. There's nothing like a schizoid lawsuit when it comes to complications and verbal quibbling. But all the same I'm grateful to you—I didn't *have* to go and save your life. I don't know quite what got into me."

"That's what got into you," Gygyo gestured at Mary Ann.

134

"The century of regimentation, of total war, of massive eavesdropping. I know: it's contagious."

Mary Ann exploded. "Well, really! I never in my life—really I—I—I just can't believe it! First, she doesn't want to save your life, because it would be interfering with your unconscious—your *unconscious*! Then, when she finally does something about it, she apologizes to you—she *apologizes*! And you, instead of thanking her, you talk as if you're excusing her for—for committing assault and battery! And then you start insulting *me*—and—and—"

"I'm sorry," Gygyo said. "I didn't intend to insult you, Mary Ann, neither you nor your century. After all, we must remember that it was the first century of modern times, it was the crisis-sickness from which recovery began. And it was in very many ways a truly great and adventuresome period, in which Man, for the last time, dared many things which he has never since attempted."

"Well. In that case." Mary Ann swallowed and began to feel better. And at that moment, she saw Gygyo and Flureet exchange the barest hint of a smile. She stopped feeling better. Damn these people! Who did they think they were?

Flureet moved to the yellow square exit. "I'll have to be going," she said. "I just stopped in to say good-bye before my transformation. Wish me luck, Gygyo."

"Your transformation? So soon? Well, all the best of course. It's been good knowing you, Flureet."

When the woman had left, Mary Ann looked at Gygyo's deeply concerned face and asked hesitantly: "What does she mean—'transformation?' And she said it was a *major* transformation. I haven't heard of that so far."

The dark-haired young man studied the wall for a moment. "I'd better not," he said at last, mostly to himself. "That's one of the concepts you'd find upsetting, like our active food for instance. And speaking of food—I'm hungry. Hungry, do you hear? *Hungry!*"

A section of the wall shook violently as his voice rose. It protruded an arm of itself at him. A tray was balanced on the end of the arm. Still standing, Gygyo began to eat from the tray.

He didn't offer Mary Ann any, which, as far as she was concerned, was just as well. She had seen at a glance that it was the purple spaghetti-like stuff of which he was so terribly fond.

Maybe it tasted good. Maybe it didn't. She'd never know. She only knew that she could never bring herself to eat anything which squirmed upwards toward one's mouth and wriggled about cozily once it was inside.

That was another thing about this world. The things these people *ate!*

Gygyo glanced up and saw her face. "I wish you'd try it just once, Mary Ann," he said wistfully. "It would add a whole new dimension to food for you. In addition to flavor, texture and aroma, you'd experience *motility*. Think of it: food not just lying there limp and lifeless in your mouth, but food expressing eloquently its desire to be eaten. Even your friend, Winthrop, culinary esthete that he is, admitted to me the other day that Centaurian *libalilil* has it all over his favorite food symphonies in many ways. You see, they're mildly telepathic and can adjust their flavor to the dietary wishes of the person consuming them. That way, you get—"

"Thank you, but *please!* It makes me absolutely and completely sick even to think of it."

"All right." He finished eating, nodded at the wall. The wall withdrew the arm and sucked the tray back into itself. "I give up. All I wanted was to have you sample the stuff before you left. Just a taste."

"Speaking of leaving, that's what I came to see you about. We're having trouble."

"Oh, Mary Ann! I was hoping you'd come to see me for myself alone," he said with a disconsolate droop of his head.

She couldn't tell whether he was being funny or serious; she got angry as the easiest way of handling the situation. "See here, Gygyo Rablin, you are the very last man on Earth —past, present, or future—that I ever want to see again. And you know why! Any man who—who says things to a girl like you said to m-me, and at s-such a t-time. . ."

Against her will, and to her extreme annoyance, her voice broke. Tears burst from her eyelids and itched their way down her face. She set her lips determinedly and tried to shake them away.

Gygyo looked really uncomfortable now. He sat down on a corner of the desk which squirmed under him more erratically than ever.

"I am sorry, Mary Ann. Truly, terribly, sincerely sorry. I should never have made love to you in the first place. Even without our substantial temporal and cultural differences, I'm certain that you know, as well as I do, we have precious little in common. But I found you—well, enormously attractive, overpoweringly attractive. I found you exciting like no woman in my own time, or any woman that I've ever encountered in a visit to the future. I just couldn't resist the attraction. The one thing I didn't anticipate was the depressing

136

effect your peculiar cosmetics would have upon me. The actual tactile sensations were extremely upsetting."

"That's not what you said. And the way you said it! You rubbed your finger on my face and lips, and you went: *'Grea-sy! Grea-sy!'* " Thoroughly in control of herself now, she mimicked him viciously.

Gygyo shrugged. "I said I'm sorry, and I meant it. But, Mary Ann, if you only know how that stuff feels to a highly educated tactile sense! That smeary red lipstick—and oh that finely-grated nonsense on your cheeks! There's no excuse for me, that I'll grant, but I'm just trying to make you understand why I erupted so stupidly."

"I suppose you think I'd be a lot nicer if I shaved my head like some of these women—like that horrible Flureet!"

He smiled and shook his head. "No, Mary Ann, you couldn't be like them, and they couldn't be like you. There are entirely different concepts of womanhood and beauty involved. In your period, the greatest emphasis is on a kind of physical similarity, the use of various artificial props which will make the woman most nearly approach a universally-agreed-upon ideal, and an ideal which consists of such items as redness of lips, smoothness of complexion and specific bodily shape. Whereas we place the accent on difference, but most particularly on *emotional* difference. The more emotions a woman can exhibit, and the more complex they are —the more striking is she considered. That's the point of the shaved heads: to show suddenly-appearing subtle wrinkles that might be missed if the area were covered with hair And that's why we call Woman's bald head her frowning glory."

Mary Ann's shoulders slumped and she stared down at the floor which started to raise a section of itself questioningly but sank back down again as it realized that nothing was required of it. "I don't understand, and I guess I won't ever understand. All I know is that I just can't stay in the same world with you, Gygyo Rablin—the very thought of it makes me feel kind of all wrong and sick inside."

"I understand," he nodded seriously. "And whatever comfort it may be—you have the same effect on me. I'd never have done anything as supremely idiotic as going on a locked micro-hunt in an impure culture before I met you. But those exciting stories of your adventuresome friend Edgar Rapp finally crept under my skin. I found I had to prove myself a man, in your terms, Mary Ann, in *your* terms!"

"Edgar *Rapp?*" she raised her eyes and looked at him incredulously. "Adventuresome? Exciting? *Edgar?* The only time *he* ever gets close to sport is when he sits on his behind all night playing poker with the boys in the payroll department!"

Gygyo rose and ambled about the room aimlessly, shaking his head. "The way you say it, the casual, half-contemptuous way you say it! The constant psychic risks run, the inevitably recurring clashes of personality—subliminal and overt—as hand after hand is played, as hour after hour goes by, with not two, not three, but as many as five, six or even seven, different and highly aggressive human beings involved—The bluffs, the raises, the outwitting, the fantastic contest of it! And to you these things are almost nothing, they're no more than what you'd expect of a masculine man! I couldn't face it; in fact, there is not a man in my entire world who'd be able to stand up to fifteen minutes of such complex psychological punishment."

Her gaze was very soft and tender as she watched him knock unhappily about the room. "And that's why you went into that awful microscope, Gygyo? To prove that you could be as good a man as Edgar is when he's playing poker?"

"It's not just the poker, Mary Ann. That's hair-raising enough, I grant you. It's so many things. Take this used car he has, that he drives you around in. Any man who'd drive one of those clumsy, unpredictable power-plants through the kind of traffic and the kind of accident statistics that your world boasts— *And every day, as a matter of course!* I knew the micro-hunt was a pathetic, artificial affair, but it was the only thing available to me that even came close!"

"You don't have to prove anything to me, Gygyo."

"Maybe I don't," he brooded. "But I had reached the point where I had to prove it to myself. Which is quite silly when you come to think of it, but that doesn't make it any less real. And I proved something after all. That two people with entirely different standards for male and female, standards that have been postulated and recapitulated for them since infancy, don't have a chance, no matter how attractive they find each other. I can't live with my knowledge of your innate standards, and you—well, you certainly have found mine upsetting. We don't mesh, we don't resonate, we don't *go*. As you said before, we shouldn't be in the same world. That's doubly true ever since—well, ever since we found out how strongly we tend to come together."

Mary Ann nodded. "I know. The way you stopped making love to me, and—and said—that horrid word, the way you kind of shuddered when you wiped your lips—Gygyo, you looked at me as if I stank, as if I *stank*! It tore me absolutely and completely to bits. I knew right then I had to get

138

out of your time and out of your universe forever. But with Winthrop acting the way he is—I don't know what to do!"

"Tell me about it." He seemed to make an effort to pull himself together as he sat beside her on a section of upraised floor.

By the time she had finished, his recovery was complete. The prodigious leveling effect of mutual emotional involvement was no longer operative. Dismayed, Mary Ann watched him becoming once more a highly urbane, extremely intelligent and slightly supercilious young man of the twenty-fifth century, and felt in her very bone marrow her own awkwardness increase, her garish, none-too-bright primitiveness come thickly to the surface.

"I can't do a thing for you," he said. "I wish I could."

"Not even," she asked desperately, "with the problems we have? Not even considering how terrible it'll be if I stay here, if I don't leave on time?"

"Not even considering all that. I doubt that I could make it clear to you, however much I tried, Mary Ann, but I can't force Winthrop to go, I can't in all conscience give you any advice on how to force him—and I can't think of a thing that would make him change his mind. You see there's a whole social fabric involved which is far more significant than our personal little agonies, however important they may be to us. In my world, as Storku pointed out, one just doesn't do such things. And that, my sweet, is that."

Mary Ann sat back. She hadn't needed the slightly mocking hauteur of Gygyo's last words to tell her that he was now completely in control of himself, that once more he was looking upon her as an intriguing but—culturally speaking—extremely distant specimen.

She knew only too well what was happening: she'd been on the other end of this kind of situation once or twice herself. Just two months ago, a brilliantly smooth salesman, who handled the Nevada territory for her company, had taken her out on a date and almost swept her off her feet.

Just as she'd reached the point where the wine in her brain was filled with bubbles of starlight, she'd taken out a cigarette and dreamily, helplessly, asked him for a light. The salesman had clicked a lighter at her in an assured and lordly gesture, but the lighter had failed to work. He had cursed, clicked it futilely a few more times, then had begun picking at the mechanism madly with his fingernails. In the next few moments as he continued to claw at the lighter, it had seemed to Mary Ann that the glossy surface of his personality developed an enormous fisure along its entire length and all the underlying desperation that was essentially him leaked out. He was no longer a glamorous, successful and warmly persuasive young man, but a pathetically driven creature who was overpoweringly uncertain, afraid that if one item in his carefully prepared presentation missed its place in the schedule, the sale would not take place.

And it didn't. When he'd looked at her again, he saw the cool comprehension in her eyes; his lips sagged. And no matter how wittily he tried to recapture the situation, how cleverly he talked, how many oceans of sparkling urgency he washed over her, she was his master now. She had seen through his magic to the unhooded yellow light bulbs and the twisted, corroded wires which made it work. She remembered feeling somewhat sorry for him as she'd asked him to take her home—not sorry for someone with whom she'd almost fallen in love, but slight sorrow for a handicapped child (someone else's handicapped child) who had tried to do something utterly beyond his powers.

Was that what Gygyo was feeling for her now? With brimming anger and despair, Mary Ann felt she had to reach him again, reach him very personally. She had to wipe that smile off his eyelids.

"Of course," she said, selecting the first arrow that came to hand, "it won't do you any good if Winthrop doesn't go back with us."

He looked at her questioningly. "Me?"

"Well, if Winthrop doesn't go back, we'll be stuck here. And if we're stuck here, the people from your time who are visiting ours will be stuck in the twentieth century. You're the temporal supervisor—you're responsible, aren't you? You might lose your job."

"My dear little Mary Ann! I can't lose my job. It's mine till I don't want it any more. Getting fired—what a concept! Next you'll be telling me I'm liable to have my ears cropped!"

To her chagrin, he chuckled all over his shoulders. Well, at least she had put him in a good mood; no one could say that she hadn't contributed to this hilarity. And *My dear little Mary Ann*. That stung!

"Don't you even *feel* responsible? Don't you feel anything?"

"Well, whatever I feel, it certainly isn't responsible. The five people from this century who volunteered to make the trip back to yours were well-educated, extremely alert, highly responsible human beings. They knew they were running certain inevitable risks."

She rose agitatedly. "But how were they to know that

Winthrop was going to be stubborn? And how could we, Gygyo, how could we know that?"

"Even assuming that the possibility entered nobody's mind," he pointed out, tugging at her arm gently until she sat down beside him again, "one has to, in all reason, admit that transferring to a period five centuries distant from one's own must be accompanied by certain dangers. Not being able to return is one of them. Then, one has to further admit that, this being so, one or more of the people making the transfer recognized this danger—at least unconsciously—and wished to subject themselves to its consequences. If this is at all the situation, interference would be a major crime, not only against Winthrop's conscious desires, but against such people's unconscious motivations as well—and both have almost equal weight in the ethics of our period. There! That's about as simple as I can make it, Mary Ann. Do you understand, now?"

"A—a little," she confessed. "You mean it's like Flureet not wanting to save you when you were almost being killed in that micro-hunt, because maybe, unconsciously, you *wanted* to get yourself killed?"

"Right! And believe me, Flureet wouldn't have lifted a finger, old friend or no old friend, your romantic twentieth-century dither notwithstanding, if she hadn't been on the verge of major transformation with the concurrent psychological remove from all normal standards and present-day human frames of reference."

"What *is* this major transformation business?"

Gygyo shook his head emphatically. "Don't ask me that. You wouldn't understand it, you wouldn't like it—and it's not at all important for you to know. It's a concept and a practice as peculiar to our time as, oh say, tabloid journalism and election night excitement is to yours. What you want to appreciate is this other thing—the way we protect and nurture the individual eccentric impulse, even if it should be suicidal. Let me put it this way. The French Revolution tried to sum itself up in the slogan, *Liberté, Egalité, Fraternité;* The American Revolution used the phrase, Life, Liberty and the Pursuit of Happiness. We feel that the entire concept of our civilization is contained in these words: The Utter Sacredness of the Individual and the Individual Eccentric Impulse. The last part is the most important, because without it our society would have as much right to interfere with the individual as yours did; a man wouldn't even have the elementary freedom of doing away with himself without getting the proper papers filled out by the proper government official. A person who wanted to—"

Mary Ann stood up with determination. "All right! I'm not the least little bit interested in this nonsense. You won't help us in any way, you don't care if we're stuck here for the rest of our natural lives, and that's that! I might as well go."

"In the name of the covenant, girl, what did you *expect* me to tell you? I'm no Oracle Machine. I'm just a man."

"A man?" she cried scornfully. "A man? You call yourself a man? Why, a man would—a man would—a real man would just— Oh, let me get out of here!"

The dark-haired young man shrugged and rose too. He called for a jumper. When it materialized beside them, he gestured toward it courteously. Mary Ann started for it, paused, and held out a hand to him.

"Gygyo," she said, "whether we stay or leave on time, I'm never going to see you again. I've made up my mind on that. But there's one thing I want you to know."

As if knowing what she was going to say, he had dropped his eyes. His head was bent over the hand he had taken.

Seeing this, Mary Ann's voice grew gentler and more tender. "It's just—just that—oh, Gygyo, it's that you're the only man I've ever loved. Ever really truly, absolutely and completely loved. I want you to know that, Gygyo."

He didn't reply. He was still holding her fingers tightly, and she couldn't see his eyes.

"Gygyo," she said her voice breaking. "Gygyo! You're feeling the same, aren't—"

At last Gygyo looked up. There was an expression of puzzlement on his face. He pointed to the fingers he had been holding. The nail of each one was colored with a bright lacquer.

"Why in the world," he asked, "do you limit it to the fingernail? Most primitive peoples who went in for this sort of thing did it on other and larger parts of the body. One would expect that at least you would tattoo the whole hand — Mary Ann! Did I say anything wrong again?"

Sobbing bitterly, the girl darted past him and into the jumper.

She went back to Mrs. Brucks' room, and, when she had been calmed sufficiently, explained why Gygyo Rablin, the temporal supervisor, either could not or would not help them with Winthrop's stubbornness.

Dave Pollock glared around the oval room. "So we give up? Is that what it comes down to? Not one person in all this brilliant, gimmicky, gadgety future will lift a finger to help us get back to our own time and our own families—

142

and we can't help ourselves. A brave new world, all right. Real achievement. Real progress."

"I don't see what call you have to shoot your mouth off, young man," Mr. Mead muttered from where he was sitting at the far end of the room. Periodically, his necktie curled upwards and tried to nuzzle against his lips; wearily, petulantly, he slapped it down again. "At least we tried to do something about it. That's more than you can say."

"Ollie, old boy, you just tell me something I can do, and I'll do it. I may not pay a whopping income tax, but I've been trained to use my mind. I'd like nothing better than to find out what a thoroughly rational approach to this problem could do for us. One thing I know: it can't possible come up with less than all this hysteria and emotional hoop-la, this flag-waving and executive-type strutting have managed to date."

"Listen, a difference it makes?" Mrs. Brucks held her wrist out and pointed to the tiny, gold-plated watch strapped around it. "Only forty-five minutes left before six o'clock. So what can we do in forty-five minutes? A miracle maybe we can manufacture on short notice? Magic we can turn out to order? Go fight City Hall. My Barney I know I won't see again."

The thin young man turned on her angrily. "I'm not talking of magic and miracles. I'm talking of logic. Logic and the proper evaluation of data. These people not only have a historical record available to them that extends back to and includes our own time, but they are in regular touch with the future—their future. That means there are also available to them historical records that extend back to and include *their* time."

Mrs. Brucks cheered up perceptibly. She liked listening to education. She nodded. "So?"

"Isn't it obvious? Those people who exchanged with us— our five opposite numbers—they must have known in advance that Winthrop was going to be stubborn. Historical records to that effect existed in the future. They wouldn't have done it—it stands to reason they wouldn't want to spend the rest of their lives in what is for them a pretty raw and uncivilized environment—unless they had known of a way out, a way that the situation could be handled. It's up to us to find that way."

"Maybe," Mary Ann Carthington suggested, bravely biting the end off a sniffle, "Maybe the next future kept it a secret from them. Or maybe all five of them were suffering from what they call here a bad case of individual eccentric impulse."

"That's not how the concept of individual eccentric impulse works, Mary Ann," Dave Pollock told her with a contemptuous grimace. "I don't want to go into it now, but *believe me,* that's not how it works! And I don't think the temporal embassies keep this kind of secret from the people in the period to which they're accredited. No, I tell you the solution is right here if we can only see it."

Oliver T. Mead had been sitting with an intent expression on his face, as if he were trying to locate a fact hidden at the other end of a long tunnel of unhappiness. He straightened up suddenly and said: "Storku mentioned that! The Temporal Embassy. But he didn't think it was a good idea to approach them—they were too involved with long-range historical problems to be of any use to us. But something else he said—something else we could do. What was it, now?"

They all looked at him and waited anxiously while he thought. Dave Pollock had just begun a remark about "high surtax memories" when the rotund executive clapped his hands together resoundingly.

"I remember! The Oracle Machine! He said we could ask the Oracle Machine. We might have some difficulty interpreting the answer, according to him, but at this point that's the least of our worries. We're in a desperate emergency, and beggars can't be choosers. If we get any kind of answer, any kind of an answer at all. . . ."

Mary Ann Carthington looked away from the tiny cosmetics laboratory she was using to repair the shiny damage caused by tears. "Now that you bring it up, Mr. Mead, the temporal supervisor made some such remark to me, too. About the Oracle Machine, I mean."

"He did? Good! That firms it up nicely. We may still have a chance, ladies and gentlemen, we may still have a chance. Well then, as to who shall do it. I am certain I don't have to draw a diagram when it comes to selecting the one of us most capable of dealing with a complex piece of futuristic machinery."

They all stared at Dave Pollock who swallowed hard and inquired hoarsely, "You mean me?"

"Certainly I mean you, young man," Mr. Mead said sternly. "You're the long-haired scientific expert around here. You're the chemistry and physics professor."

"I'm a teacher, that's all, a high-school science *teacher.* And you know how I feel about having anything to do with the Oracle Machine. Even the thought of getting close to it makes my stomach turn over. As far as I'm concerned it's

144

the one aspect of this civilization that's most horrible, most decadent. Why, I'd rather—"

"My stomach didn't turn over when I had to go in and have an argument with that crazy Mr. Winthrop?" Mrs. Brucks broke in. "Till then, out of this room I hadn't taken a step, with all the everything I had positively nothing to do —you think I liked watching one minute a pair of rompers, the next minute, I don't know what, an evening gown he starts wearing? And that crazy talk he talks—smell this from a Mars, taste this from a Venus—you think maybe, Mr. Pollock, I enjoyed myself? But somebody had to do, so I did. All we're asking you is a try. A try you can make?"

"And I can assure you," Mary Ann Carthington came on in swiftly, "that Gygyo Rablin is absolutely and completely the last person on Earth I would go to for a favor. It's a personal matter, and I'd rather not discuss it now, if you don't mind, but I would die, positively *die*, rather than go through that again. I did it though, because there was the teensiest chance it would help us all get home again. I don't think we're asking too much of you, I don't think so one little bit."

Mr. Mead nodded. "I agree with you, young lady. Storku is a man I haven't seen eye to eye with since we've arrived, and I've gone out of my way to avoid him, but to have to get involved in that unholy Shriek Field madness in the bargain—" He brooded for a while over some indigestible mental fragment, then, as his cleated golf shoes began squirming lovingly about on his feet, shook himself determinedly and went on: "It's about time you stopped shooting off your mouth, Pollock, and got down to humdrum, specific brass tacks. Einstein's theory of relativity isn't going to get us back to good old 1958, and neither is your Ph.D. or M.A. or whatever. What we need now is action, action with a capital *A* and no ifs, no ands, no buts."

"All right, all right. I'll do it."

"And another thing." Mr. Mead rolled a wicked little thought pleasurably to and fro in his mind for a moment or two before letting it out. "You take the jumper. You said yourself we don't have the time to do any walking, and that's doubly true right now, doubly true, when we're right up against the dead, dead deadline. I don't want to hear any whining and any whimpering about it making you sick. If Miss Carthington and I could take the jumper, so can you."

In the midst of his misery, Dave Pollock rallied. "You think I won't?" he asked scornfully. "I've done most of my

145

traveling here by jumper. I'm not afraid of mechanical progress—just so long as it's genuine *progress*. Of course I'll take the jumper."

He signaled for one with a microscopic return of his old swagger. When it appeared, he walked under it with squared shoulders. Let them all watch how a rational, scientifically-minded man goes about things, he thought. And anyway, using the jumper wasn't nearly as upsetting to him as it seemed to be to the others. He could take jumpers in stride.

Which was infinitely more than he could say for the Oracle Machine.

For that reason, he had himself materialized outside the building which housed the machine. A bit of a walk and he might be able to get his thoughts in order.

The only trouble was, the sidewalk had other ideas. Silently, obsequiously, but nonetheless firmly, it began to move under his feet as he started walking around the squat, slightly quivering structure. It rippled him ahead at a pace somewhat faster than the one he set, changing direction as soon as he changed his.

Dave Pollock looked around at the empty streets and smiled with resignation. The sentient, eager-to-serve sidewalks didn't bother him, either. He had expected something like that in the future, that and the enormously alert servitor houses, the clothes which changed their color and cut at the wearers' caprice—all more or less, in one form or another, to be anticipated, by a knowledgeable man, of human progress. Even the developments in food—from the wriggling, telepathic, please-eat-me-and-enjoy-me stuff all the way up to the more complex culinary compositions on which an interstellarly famous chef might have worked for a year or more—was logical, if you considered how bizarre to an early American colonist, would be the fantastic, cosmopolitan variety of potables and packaged meals available in any twentieth-century supermarket.

These things, the impediments of daily life, all change and modify in time. But certain things, *certain* things, should not.

When the telegram had arrived in Houston, Texas, informing him that—of all the people in the United States of America—he was most similar in physical composition and characteristics to one of the prospective visitors from 2458 A.D., he had gone almost mad with joy. The celebrity he suddenly enjoyed in the faculty lunchroom was unimportant, as were the Page One stories in local newspapers under the heading: LONE STAR SON GALLOPING FUTUREWARDS.

First and foremost, it was reprieve. It was reprieve and another chance. Family responsibilities, a dying father, a sick

146

younger sister, had prevented him from getting the advanced academic degrees necessary for a university teaching position with all of its accompanying prestige, higher income and opportunities for research. Then, when they had come to an end and he had gone back to school, a sudden infatuation and too-hasty marriage had thrown him back onto the same treadmill. He had just begun to realize—despite the undergraduate promise he had shown and none-too-minute achievement—how thoroughly he was trapped by the pleasant residential neighborhood and cleanly modern high school between which he shuttled daily, when the telegram arrived, announcing his selection as one of the group to be sent five hundred years ahead. How it was going to help him, what, precisely, he would do with the chance, he did not know—but it had lifted him out of the ruck of anonymity; somehow, someway, it would enable him to become a striking individual at last.

Dave Pollock had not realized the extent of his good fortune until he met the other four in Washington, D. C. He had heard, of course, how the finest minds in the country had bitterly jostled and elbowed each other in a frenzied attempt to get into the group and find out what was going to develop in *their* speciality half a millenium hence. But not until he had talked with his prospective fellow-tourists—an itinerant worker, a Bronx housewife, a pompous mid-western business executive, a pretty but otherwise very ordinary San Francisco stenographer—did it come to him that he was the only one with any degree of scientific training.

He would be the only one capable of evaulating the amount of major technological advance! He would be the only one to correlate all the bewildering mass of minor changes into something resembling coherence! And thus, above all, he would be the only one to appreciate the essential quality of the future, the basic threads that would run through it from its underlying social fabric to its star-leaping fringes!

He, who had wanted to devote his life to knowledge-seeking, would exist for two weeks, unique and intellectually alone, in a five-century-long extrapolation of every laboratory and library in his age!

At first, it had been like that. Everywhere there was glory and excitement and discovery. Then, little, disagreeable things began to creep in, like the first stages of a cold. The food, the clothing, the houses—well, you either ignored it or made other arrangements. These people were extremely hospitable and quite ingenious: they didn't at all mind providing you with more familiar meals when your intestines had revolted a couple of times. The women, with their glossy bald-

147

ness and strange attitudes toward relations between the sexes —well, you had a brand-new wife at home and didn't have to get involved with the women.

But Shriek Field, Panic Stadium, that was another matter. Dave Pollock was proud of being a thoroughly rational person. He had been proud of the future, when he first arrived, taking it almost as a personal vindication that the people in it should be so thoroughly, universally rational, too. His first acquaintance with Shriek Field had almost nauseated him. That the superb intellects he had come to know should *willingly* transform themselves into a frothing, hysterical pack of screaming animals, and at regular, almost medically-prescribed intervals. . . .

They had explained to him painfully, elaborately, that they could not be such superb intellects, so thoroughly rational, unless they periodically released themselves in this fashion. It made sense, but—still—*watching* them do it was absolutely horrifying. He knew he would never be able to stand the sight of it.

Still, this one could make acceptable in some corner of the brain. But the chess business?

Since his college days, Dave Pollock had fancied himself as a chess player. He was just good enough to be able to tell himself that if ever he had the time to really concentrate on the game, to learn the openings, say, as they should be learned, he'd be good enough to play in tournaments. He'd even subscribed to a chess magazine and followed all the championship matches with great attention. He'd wondered what chess would be like in the future—surely the royal game having survived for so many centuries would survive another five? What would it be like: a version of three-dimensional chess, or possibly another, even more complex evolution?

The worst of it was the game was almost identical with the one played in the twentieth century.

Almost every human being in 2458 played it; almost every human being in 2458 enjoyed it. But there were no human champions. There were no human opponents.

There were only the chess machines. And they could beat anybody.

"What's the sense," he had wailed, "of playing with a machine which has millions of 'best moves and counter-moves' built into its memory circuits? That has a selector mechanism able to examine and choose from every chess game ever recorded? A machine which has been *designed* never to be beaten? What's the sense—where's the excitement?

"We don't play to win," they had explained wonderingly. "We play to play. It's the same with all our games: aggressions are gotten rid of in a Shriek or a Panic, games are just for mental or physical exercise. And so, when we play, we want to play against the best. Besides, every once in a while, an outstandingly good player, once or twice in his lifetime, is able to hold the machine to a draw. Now, *that* is an achievement. *That* merits excitement."

You had to love chess as much as he did, Dave Pollock supposed, to realize what an obscenity the existence of these machines made of it. Even the other three in his group, who had become much more restive than he at twenty-fifth century mechanisms and mores, only stared at him blankly when he raged over it. No, if you didn't love something, you weren't bothered overmuch when it was degraded. But surely they could see the abdication of human intellect, of human reason, that the chess machines implied?

Of course, that was nothing compared to the way human reason had abdicated before the Oracle Machine. That was the last, disgusting straw to a rational person.

The Oracle Machine. He glanced at his watch. Only twenty-five minutes left. Better hurry. He took one last self-encouraging breath and climbed the cooperative steps of the building.

"My name is Stilia," a bald-headed, rather pleasant-faced young woman said as she came toward him in the spacious ante-room. "I'm the attendant of the machine for today. Can I help you?"

"I suppose so." He looked uncomfortably at a distant, throbbing wall. Behind the yellow square on that well, he knew, was the inner brain of the Oracle Machine. How he'd love to kick a hole in that brain!

Instead, he sat down on an upraised hummock of floor and wiped his perspiring hands carefully. He told her about their approaching deadline, about Winthrop's stubbornness, about the decision to consult the Oracle Machine.

"Oh, Winthrop, yes! He's that delightful old man. I met him at a dream dispensary a week ago. What wonderful awareness he has! Such a total immersion in our culture! We're very proud of Winthrop. We'd like to help him every way we possibly can."

"If you don't mind, lady," Dave Pollock said morosely, "we're the ones who need help. We've *got* to get back."

Stilia laughed. "Of course. We'd like to help everybody. Only Winthrop is—*special*. He's trying hardest. Now, if you'll just wait here, I'll go in and put your problem before the Oracle Machine. I know how to do it so that it will activate the relevant memory circuits with the least loss of time."

She flexed her right arm at him and walked toward the

yellow square. Pollock watched it expand in front of her, then, as she went through the opening it made, contract behind her. In a few minutes she returned.

"I'll tell you when to go in, Mr. Pollock. The machine is working on your problem. The answer you get will be the very best that can be made, given the facts available."

"Thanks." He thought for a while. "Tell me something. Doesn't it seem to take something out of life—out of your thinking life—to know that you can take absolutely any problem, personal problem, scientific problem or working problem, to the Oracle Machine and it will solve it much better than you could?"

Stilia looked puzzled. "Not at all. To begin with, problem-solving is a very small part of today's thinking life. It would be as logical to say that it took something vital out of life to make a hole with an electric drill instead of a hand drill. In your time, no doubt, there are people who feel just that way, they have the obvious privilege of not using electric drills. Those who use electric drills, however, have their physical energy freed for tasks they regard as more important. The Oracle Machine is the major tool of our culture; it has been designed toward just one end—computing all the factors of a given problem and relating them to the totality of pertinent data that is in the possession of the human race. But even if people consult the Oracle Machine, they may not be able to understand and apply the answer. And, if they do understand it, they may not choose to act on it."

"They may not choose to act on it? Does that make sense? You said yourself the answers are the very best that can be made, given the facts available."

"Human activities don't necessarily have to make sense. That is the prevailing and rather comfortable modern view, Mr. Pollock. There is always the individual eccentric impulse."

"Yeah, there's always that," he growled. "Resign your private, distinct personality by running with a howling mob at Shriek Field, lose all of yourself in an insane crowd—but don't forget your individual eccentric impulse. Never, *never* forget your individual eccentric impulse!"

She nodded soberly. "That really sums it up, I must say, in spite of your rather unmistakable sarcasm. Why do you find it so hard to accept? Man is both a herd animal and a highly individualistic animal—what we call a self-realizable animal. The herd instincts must be satisfied at whatever cost, and have been in the past through such mechanisms as warfare, religion, nationalism, partyism and various forms of group chauvinism. The need to resign one's personality and immerse in something larger than self has been recognized since

150

earliest times: Shriek Fields and Panic Stadiums everywhere on the planet provide for this need and expend it harmlessly."

"I wouldn't say it was so harmless from the look of that mechanical rabbit, or whatever it was."

"I understand that human beings who took the place of the mechanical rabbit in the past looked much worse when a herd of men was through with them," she suggested, locking eyes with him. "Yes, Mr. Pollock, I think you know what I mean. The self-realizable instincts, on the other hand, must be satisfied, too. Usually, they can be satisfied in terms of one's daily life and work, as the herd instincts can be fulfilled by normal group relationships and identification with humanity. But occasionally, the self-realizable instincts must be expressed at abnormal strengths, and then we have to have a kind of private Shriek Field—the concept of individual eccentric impulse. The two are opposite poles of exactly the same thing. All we require is that another human being will not be actively interfered with."

"And so long as that doesn't happen, *anything* goes!"

"Exactly. Anything goes. Absolutely anything a person may want to do out of his own individual eccentric impulse is permitted. Encouraged, actually. It's not only that we consider that some of humanity's greatest achievements have come out of individual eccentric impulses, but that we feel the greatest glory of our civilization is the homage we pay to such intrinsically personal expression."

Dave Pollock stared at her with reluctant respect. She was bright. This was the kind of girl he might have married if he'd gone on to his doctorate, instead of Susie. Although Susie— He wondered if he'd ever see Susie again. He was astonished at how bitterly homesick he felt.

"It sounds good," he admitted. "But living with it is another thing entirely. I guess I'm too much a product of my own culture to ever swallow it down all the way. I can't get over how much difference there is between our civilizations. We talk the same language but we sure as hell don't think the same thoughts."

Stilia smiled warmly and sat back. "One of the reasons your period was invited to exchange visitors with us is because it was the first in which most speech patterns became constant and language shifts came to an end. Your newly-invented speech recording devices were responsible for that. But technological progress continued, and sociological progress actually accelerated. Neither was solidified to any great extent until the invention in the latter part of the twenty-third century—"

A hum began in the distant wall. Stilia broke off and stood

up. "The Oracle Machine is ready to give you the answer to your problem. Just go inside, sit down and repeat your question in its simplest form. I wish you well."

I wish me well, too, Dave Pollock thought, as he went through the dilated yellow square and into the tiny cube of a room. For all of Stilia's explication, he was supremely uncomfortable in this world of simply satisfied herd instincts and individual eccentric impulses. He was no misfit; he was no Winthrop: he very much wanted out and to return to what was smoothly familiar.

Above all, he didn't want to stay any longer in a world where almost any question he might think of would be answered best by the blueish, narrow, throbbing walls which surrounded him.

But— He did have a problem he couldn't solve. And this machine could.

He sat down. "What do we do about Winthrop's stubbornness?" he asked, idiotically feeling like a savage interrogating a handful of sacred bones.

A deep voice, neither masculine nor feminine in quality, rumbled from the four walls, from the ceiling, from the floor.

"You will go to the time travel bureau in the Temporal Embassy at the proper time."

He waited. Nothing more was forthcoming. The walls were still.

The Oracle Machine evidently had not understood.

"It won't do us any good to be there," he pointed out. "Winthrop is stubborn, he won't go back with us. And, unless all five of us go back together, none of us can go. That's the way the transferring device is set. So, what I want to know is, how do we persuade Winthrop without—"

Again the enormous voice.

"You will go to the time travel bureau in the Temporal Embassy at the proper time."

And that seemed to be that.

Dave Pollock trudged out and told Stilia what had happened. "It seems to me," he commented just a little nastily, "that the machine found the problem was just a bit too much for it and was trying hard to change the subject."

"Just the same, I would do what it advised. Unless, of course, you find another, subtler interpretation of the answer."

"Or unless my individual eccentric impulse gets in the way?"

This time the sarcasm was lost on her. She opened her eyes wide. "That would be best of all! Imagine if you should at last learn to exercise it!"

So Dave Pollock went back to Mrs. Brucks's room and, thoroughly exasperated, told the others of the ridiculous answer the Oracle Machine had given him on the problem of Winthrop's stubbornness.

At a few minutes to six, however, all four of them—Mrs. Brucks, Oliver T. Mead, Mary Ann Carthington, Dave Pollock—were in the time-travel bureau of the Temporal Embassy, having arrived in varying stages of upset by way of jumper. They didn't have any particular hopes: there just wasn't anything else to do.

They sat dispiritedly in their transfer seats and stared at their watches.

At precisely one minute to six, a large group of twenty-fifth century citizens came in to the transfer room. Gygyo Rablin, the temporal supervisor, was among them, as was Stilia the attendant of the Oracle Machine, Flureet, wearing the drawn look of one awaiting major transformation, Mr. Storku, returned temporarily from the Odor Festival on Venus—and many, many others. They carried Winthrop to his proper seat and stood back with reverent expressions on their faces. They looked like people who had seen the fulfillment of a religious ceremony—and they had.

The transfer began.

Winthrop was an old man, sixty-four, to be exact. He had, in the past two weeks, undergone much excitement. He had been on micro-hunts, undersea hunts, teleported jaunts to incredibly distant planets, excursions, numerous and fantastic. He had had remarkable things done to his body, spectacular things done to his mind. He had pounded in pursuit at Shriek Field, scuttled fearfully at Panic Stadium. And, above all, he had eaten plentifully and repeatedly of foods grown in distant stellar systems, of dishes prepared by completely alien entities, of meals whose composition had been totally unsuspected by his metabolism in the period of its maturing. He had not grown up with these things, with this food, as had the people of the twenty-fifth century: it had all been shatteringly new to his system.

No wonder they had observed with such pleased astonishment his individual eccentric impulse assert itself. No wonder they had guarded its unfolding so lovingly.

Winthrop was no longer stubborn. Winthrop was dead.

SCIENCE FICTION READERS!

NOW—you can order your favorite
Science Fiction editions . . .
DIRECTLY from the Publisher!

Have you missed any of these hard-to-get time and space BESTSELLERS?

Check the titles you wish; list your name and address; and enclose the cost of your order (sorry, no C.O.D.'s). Mail to:

BANTAM BOOKS, INC.

Dept. Z-1; 657 W. Chicago Ave.   Chicago 10, Illinois

Bantam Books are available at newsstands everywhere